'Firstborn' and Other Tales and Poems of Horror:

A Collection of Twelve Stories and Twelve Poems

E. W. Farnsworth

'Firstborn' and Other Tales and Poems of Horror:

A Collection of Twelve Stories and Twelve Poems

E. W. Farnsworth

ISBN 9798857992012

Published by AudioArcadia.com 2023

ACKNOWLEDGEMENTS

The following six stories first appeared in *The Tightfisted Scot Advisory Newsletter*. They are published herein by the express permission of Wilson F. Engel, III, Ph.D., publisher and editor of TFS: 'The Hamadryad,' 'The Carrier,' 'The Great Rift's Revenge,' 'Halloween on the Escher Highway,' 'The Music Master on North Eleventh Street" and "High-Diving Mules.'

The flash fiction story, 'Existential Pumpkin,' was first published in *Black Noise Magazine*, Issue #7 in August, 2022 and is included herein by the express permission of Josef Desade, Publisher and Editor-in-Chief.

The story, 'Treasure Hunter,' first appeared in *The Dead Game: A Collection of Horrors Anthology*, published by Zimbell House Publishing LLC in April 2020 and is included herein with the express (blanket) permission of Evelyn Zimmer, editor and publisher.

The poem, 'Deceptive Cadence,' was first published in *Dead on a Doorstop*, New Ventures Issue #26 (July 2022) and is included herein by the express permission of Josef Desade, Publisher and Editor-in-Chief.

The poem, 'Incisors Minding,' was first published in *Dead on a Doorstop*, Penultimate Issue #26 (August 2022) and is included herein by the express permission of Josef Desade, Publisher and Editor-in-Chief.

The poem, 'Deep Black Water,' was first published in *Dead on a Doorstop*, New Ventures Issue #25 (April 2022) and was subsequently published in *Black Noise Magazine* Web Exclusive Issue #20 (September

2023) and is included herein by the express permission of Josef Desade, Publisher and Editor-in-Chief.

The poem, 'No Kissing,' was first published in Eber & Wein's *Best Poets of 2019*.

The poem, 'Cut Short on the Short Cut,' was first published in The Moonlit Path Halloween Anthology, *Moonlit Path Online Magazine* (October 2020).

CONTENTS

Page No.

FOREWORD

My last published collection of horror tales was 'The Black Marble Griffon' and Other Disturbing Tales (2016), which is still available for purchase from Amazon. I continued to publish horror since then in individual stories and poems in a wide variety of congenial vehicles.

An addition to my repertoire of horror was cosmic horror, chiefly known through the works of H. P. Lovecraft and his friends—my works being sponsored by the inimitable Gavin Chappell. In this line came four years of serialized cosmic horror for *Schlock! Webzine* in *The Picklock Lane Stories*. This extremely popular, continuing series, is being published in three (or perhaps four) volumes, by AudioArcadia.com in the UK.

My so-called 'Exoteric' cosmic horror tales (whose name was taken from the title of the first story of their kind) are appearing sporadically in Gavin Chappell's other inspired monthly journal *Lovecraftiana*. The narration and setting for these tales is based roughly on my personal experiences on North Eleventh Street in Allentown, Pennsylvania, during the late Nineteen Seventies and early Eighties of the last century. The two examples of Exoteric stories included herein are 'The Music Master on North Eleventh Street' and 'High-Diving Mules.'

I am currently working on a collection devoted to the 'Exoterics,' scheduled to appear in the spring of 2025.

Meanwhile my poems come as they may of their own accord. My sincere wish is that my readers of poems and stories enjoy the games I play as much as I do writing them.

E. W. FARNSWORTH

BEACHWOOD, OHIO
SEPTEMBER 2023

BLUE STEAKS ON ST. VALENTINE'S DAY

The stock yards were full, and sounds of continual slaughter made the winter of 1880 an inauspicious time for romance. Yet at nineteen Ruth was not getting any younger, and at twenty-two, I was finally able to support a wife and family on my accountant's wages.

I met the comely counter clerk outside the entrance of the Armor Company to propose a Dutch-treat dinner the evening of February 14. I said, "Ruth, I shall meet you in the parlor of your boarding house at seven PM. We'll walk to the Stockyard Restaurant and enjoy our meal. Afterward, I'll walk you home again."

She was fussing with her gloves. "Simon, I would be happy to accept your invitation, but I cannot afford to pay for my dinner. The Stockyard Restaurant is very expensive."

I did a few calculations and changed my tactics. "Why don't I pay for both our meals? I have just enough money to cover two blue steaks, one for each of us. I won't have enough for dessert though."

She smiled. "We could split a steak. Then you'd have enough money for dessert. We'll have coffee instead of wine. I am extremely excited. I'll have the opportunity to wear the winter dress I've been sewing. You'll like it, I think. And you'll wear your brown suit?"

"That's right. I'll wear my hand-painted tie with the octopus pin you bought me for Christmas."

"I'll see you at seven on the fourteenth. You know what day that is, don't you?"

"Yes, and it is the most appropriate day for my purposes."

"Must I presume you have ulterior motives?"

"You could say that. Anyway, you've made me a happy man."

"If you say so, Simon. Good evening." Ruth

extended her gloved hand and I shook it. Then we went our separate ways in the twilight. She joined two of her fellow roomers, who had been waiting for her down the lane. I trudged homewards alone.

Black snow piled in the streets and on the walks. Snow fog rose as the lake lay calm with only a few seagulls apparent. I felt the cold through my shoes. I was warmed by the thought of our forthcoming dinner. The white fog's tentacles enveloped me. I was suddenly surrounded by five or six ruffians, who wanted my money and possibly my life.

Thieves had easy pickings amongst the salaried employees of the meat packers. They did not figure on my kind of being as a victim. I was a trained boxer and seasoned street fighter. I used the weather as a weapon. The band of brigands soon lay on all sides of me, moaning in pain. I passed by uninjured. I heard the leader of the robbers threaten me, but I did not deign to reply.

The lamplighters were busy now. They had been conspicuously absent during the above scenario. Here and there I passed constables on patrol. I heard the sounds of feet slapping on wet pavement and hooves of giant horses pulling carts with heavy loads. A sea of people immersed in fog came towards me in groups, dressed in their hats and coats, their murmurings and occasional laughter punctuating the silence as they overtook me.

I reached my rooming house in time for the evening meal. Mrs. Savage told me to take my place at the dining table and serve myself. Having divested my coat and hat, I took my usual chair and used my boarding-house reach to fill my plate.

"Mrs. Savage, I will not be at dinner on the fourteenth as I shall be dining out."

"It's good you told me, Master Floyd. The others

won't mind as there will be more for the rest of the lodgers."

The other six lodgers, four male and two female, were seated around the table, nodding their heads up and down and making animal sounds of satisfaction. One laughed outright as he stuffed his face.

The landlady handed me a second napkin and gestured for me to use it. I rubbed it against my face and, when I looked at it, I saw blood.

"I'm all right. You should see the others I put to rights." I smiled weakly.

"One day the police will be involved. Mark my words. Hooligans are taking over this city. I work hard to find civil clientele like you. I don't want to lose you."

I finished my meal, excused myself, and walked up the stairs to my room with my hat and coat in hand. There my tiny bed was ready to receive me. As my needs were few, I prepared for the evening by cleaning my teeth and washing my face. A vase with water and a bowl with a towel were sufficient. Last, I recorded my daily activities in my diary. My successful exchange with Ruth was the highlight of my week. I made no written record of the band of ruffians I had dispatched on my way home.

The last thing I did was to open a small box which contained the ring destined for Ruth's finger. I admired how the fire of the stone caught my eyes. I had been keeping the box in the inside pocket of my suit coat. On the fourteenth, the ring would either be accepted— or I would return it to the jeweler's shop for a refund.

That night as the wind howled under the gabled eaves, I slept fitfully. My mind was full of visions and dreams. I saw a tentacle creature come out of the fog to help defeat the robbers. I heard the shrill threats of the leader of the brigands. My mind's eye admired the tiepin in the shape of the octopus as if it were my talisman. As always, my accounts were my refuge. My prodigious memory retained numbers, which I checked and rechecked until I finally fell asleep.

St. Valentine's Day came with wind, rain and fog. I took one of the rooming-house umbrellas to work. I wore my painted tie and the tiepin shaped like an octopus. I padded through the thick crowd of workers. My supervisor marked my presence at the office, which was redolent of wet wool worn by the other workers. My desk held my inkwell, my account book and my goose quills. I repaired the accounts from the previous day and worked through the chits I had been allocated for recording today.

The office manager arrived at ten AM and reviewed the employees' numbers. He approved my ledger by initialing each page since his last inspection. He was about to proceed to the next employee's desk, but he hesitated as he whispered in my ear, "Two days ago, it has been alleged, you fought with six boys from our neighborhood. Their leader was the son of the chief of police. I'm aware of the sensitivity of the situation, but there is little I can do to help you. Be careful. The authorities are not to be trifled with."

I went back to my work, but I mulled over my manager's warning. I was not naïve. I did not want to lose my job or to cause my superiors trouble. I decided to take measured steps in case of unspecified difficulties. Above all, I did not need to endanger my girlfriend Ruth or my landlady Mrs. Savage.

The hours flew by, and I had closed my ledger minutes before I realized it was time to leave the office. Outside was a downpour; the streets were full of water running to the drains and the lake. This accountant had turned in the direction of Ruth's lodging when I heard the voice of the leader of the brigands: "I have come for you alone. I mean to teach you a lesson you'll never forget."

I answered, "I did not pick a fight when we last met—you did. If you come at me, I shall defend myself."

The thug advanced and threw the first punch. I evaded the blow and tripped the would-be pugilist with my umbrella. The attacker fell face downward in the rushing torrent, which transformed him into a writhing mass of tentacles forcing him underwater. The other five robbers came out of hiding to save their leader. They too became tangled in the tentacles.

Meanwhile, I continued, unscathed, on my way to Ruth's place where I met her in the parlor as we had planned at seven o'clock. She was dressed in the garment she had told me about—the one she had tailored by hand. She looked beautiful in her creation, and I told her so. She blushed bright red as she smiled.

I then told her how I had deflected the hooligan's attack with the help of an octopus. She thought I must be joking and suggested we had better walk to the restaurant. As we did so, the rain continued, and now darkness fell. Ruth lifted up the hem of her dress above the running water while I held the umbrella over us both.

The Stockyard Restaurant was packed to the gills with regular customers, but I had already reserved a table for two on the lakefront. There we ordered a blue filet mignon steak for both of us, followed by coffee and flan with white chocolate pieces for dessert. Our table featured a lighted candle and flowers. The waiter was accommodating. Ruth agreed that she had never tasted better cuisine. I assumed a kneeling position beside her at the end of the meal but before dessert and offered her the ring with my proposal of marriage.

Before she could give me her answer, two constables

13

forced their way to the table. The six ruffians were behind them, gesturing at me and egging them on to arrest me. The ruffians were joined by the chief of police, who ordered his men to take me to the police station without delay. I shrugged and asked whether I could settle my bill before we departed. While I counted out the ten dollars for the meal and tip, Ruth winked and thanked me for giving her the best time of her life.

"Somehow, I think your trip to the police station will be interrupted,' she said. 'Anyway, do as these gentlemen say. I can find my way back to my rooming house alone. And, to your question, of course, I shall marry you. We'll decide on the details later." She slipped my ring on her finger and turned back to her dessert.

I left the restaurant with one constable on each side and the police chief leading the way. I still held the umbrella high as our menagerie stepped into the running water. Tentacles rose from the stream and grasped the policemen and the brigands. In a boiling tangle of arms with suckers, the aquatic creatures pulled their prey into the lake. They did not touch me, which enabled me to return to the restaurant to escort Ruth to her lodging.

"How did you know my trip to jail would be interrupted?"

She smiled. "Give me some credit. If your account of the tentacles seizing the robbers was true, I was convinced they would protect you a second time—and they did so. If your account had been a lie which was meant to cover something you did without external aid, I was sure you would escape your predicament by yourself."

"I'm so glad you said yes!"

"I'm so glad you proposed after all these months of

anticipation."

We heard the shouting of police and robbers alike, but they were well out on the lake now. We took our time walking back to her lodging. As we stepped through the rushing water, we felt occasional tentacles rubbing against our calves and ankles.

I diverted us to a pier extending into the lake. At the pier's end, we stood as the rain ceased and the full moon shone on the placid lake. There we shared our first kiss. We stood in each other's arms until Ruth said she was getting chilly. I conducted her to her boarding house before striking for home.

I had no idea what the police chief's next move would be. I decided I would play events as they came. I resolved only that I was thankful for the tentacles that had protected me and allowed me to complete a perfect evening with my now fiancée Ruth.

FIRSTBORN

Call me Jure Grando Alilović. I am tied to Istria by tradition, but I do get around. In fact, you might find me anywhere. I can recall numerous pre-historical milestones, but they are not essential to this story. Besides, I live for the present and near-future, always. Ravenous hunger drives me, as well as my instinct for survival, which may amount to the same thing.

Today, I am a certified hematologist at the Clymer-Holster Clinic for rare blood disorders in Virginia Beach, Virginia. The job pays for the rent and a few luxuries, but it also offers a wide variety of culinary experiences in a controlled environment.

My extensive experience with the pathology of human blood systems gives me an edge over my competitors. The last two hundred years have so polluted the human blood pool with poisons and drugs, it is nigh impossible to conceive of purity in face of the egregious contaminant streams. Think of a resort with its five-star hotels pouring raw sewage into already toxic ocean water. This clinic may be a temporary refuge from some pollutants, but the nearby beaches are petri dishes for microbial growth in the same way my patients ingest and absorb pernicious nano-particulate matter and in the same fashion as the beaches on a smaller scale. Believe me, I can taste the difference between a manageable level of invasive waste and a lethal one.

My patient, Letitia Maras, who lies sedated on the gurney, is lucky. Her diagnosis of massive sepsis has been treated by a mix of antibiotics and transfusions.

After three weeks, her blood tastes normal. My razor-sharp canines slice almost imperceptibly into her neck where I feed on her blood by licking. My saliva seals her tiny wounds by the time my feeding has done.

As a rat gnaws off the extremities without pain or lasting effects in its victims, so I feast without causing forty-year-old Miss Maras discomfort or excessive blood loss. Her blood-count numbers will show improvement day-over-day as always, and her superficial presentations will prove treatable with a harmless analgesic such as aspirin. Her prognosis is therefore good. I do regret she will be de-admitted from the clinic once she has been cured. When she departs, I will be back to distasteful samplings from other, less healthy stock.

You must realize from the start I was suspicious of this vivacious young woman. An otherwise perfect physical specimen, she had bound her red hair with two suspicious wooden probes and a loop. I thought she might be a hunter-killer who had been infiltrated into my clinic to do me harm. As her medical condition could have been induced, I took extreme measures to give her no opportunities to wield her weapons—if, indeed, they were such.

Now, after three weeks, the secondary effects of my feeding should preclude her becoming hostile. Knocked out, she seems vulnerable, and her beauty is stunning. I am tempted to include her in my clutch of victims.

I need to explain. The clinic is not my *only* venue. For exceptional people, I have renovated an old barn into a lodging for twelve, of which eleven reservations are booked. Miss Maras meets all my criteria for entry *except* for my nagging feeling she may be a plant.

Others have attempted to fool me, so I am cautious to a fault about my business. Ninety-nine percent assurance leaves too much risk for my liking. With my eleven—plus myself—we have perfected our coordination for evening feedings without having to bother with an outlier.

Miss Maras seems to be stirring now.

"Miss, do you hear me? Are you conscious?"

Groggily she replies, "Yes, Dr. Alilović, I do hear you. I had the strangest feeling while I was under sedation." Her hand went to her neck where it lingered for a moment before she examined it for blood. "I dreamed I was bleeding from my neck. I suppose I am being silly."

"Miss Maras, you have nothing to worry about. I am going to stay with you until I think you can navigate properly on your own. Then you may do as you please. Three hours remain until the evening meal is served— Beef Wellington."

"That does sound good. I was hoping to take an evening jog after eating. Do you think that would be all right?"

"Exercise at any time is a good idea, as long as you don't overdo it. How far afield were you planning to roam?"

The young woman shook her head. "I don't really know. I have seen the neighborhood from my window. The beach and the woods look inviting."

"I can ask one of the orderlies to accompany you, if you wish."

"I don't think that will be necessary. The area seems safe enough, and I have martial arts skills, just in case I encounter any trouble."

I smiled at her and pressed a buzzer to summon a medical assistant. Ralph, who had once been a bouncer at a local bar, arrived immediately.

"Ralph will show you to your room, Miss Maras—or to the recreation room or to the indoor pool where you can do whatever you like."

The orderly helped the patient to get on her feet and walked beside her as they exited through the door of the examination room.

18

I made a mental note to have Ralph attach a tracking chip to Miss Maras's overcoat so I would know where she went in near-real time. Then I made my rounds to ensure my other seven patients were progressing well. Fortunately for them, none suffered emergency conditions. I used my well-received bedside manner and reminded everyone about the special dinner in store for this evening.

Ralph returned fifteen minutes later to inform me that Miss Maras was playing shuffleboard with three other female patients. I thanked him and gave him the tracking device with instructions. Straightaway he went to the young woman's closet and attached the device to her overcoat. I checked my mobile app to confirm I could receive the tracking signal. The flashing icon indicated the device was where I ordered it to be placed. I set an automatic alarm for any movement greater than twenty feet from the device's current position. I returned to my afternoon duties. Just before dinner, I checked the mobile app for another set of readings having nothing to do with those for Miss Maras. I was pleased to see the status of my clutch in the barn was unchanged.

I was looking forward to a quiet evening. My electronic monitoring systems showed medications were on schedule to be administered by the nurse practitioners and aides. As during all such peaceful intervals, my personal disposition was on high alert in anticipation of the unexpected.

At five minutes before five PM, a woman was admitted in distress, and unfortunately I had to miss the special dinner in order to attend her. I might have assigned any of my colleagues to attend to Mrs. Inez Perkins, but I saw immediately her case was beyond their ken. She was in a state of delirium and holding her neck where unmistakable signs of canine teeth marks had evidently infected the area.

I worked fast to sedate the mature woman while I ordered an IV to be placed in her arm with an antibiotic drip as she was lying in bed by this time. As the sedative took effect, the woman became somewhat articulate. She described what often occurred in classic cases of advanced transition. She spoke of an insatiable hunger deep within her soul. She was foaming at the mouth as she related her story and looked at me with a yearning I could only understand as induction.

Her open mouth bared her upper teeth. Her eyes were fluttering, appealing to me as a sympathetic being who uniquely could understand her innermost desires. She kept looking at my neck as if seeking a vantage point to bite me. Two ideas converged in my mind. First, this woman had not been affected by me or my clutch. Second, whoever had been feeding off her had been grossly remiss in respect to basic cleanliness as she needed the security of a clutch immediately.

That same evening the medical staff and other patients were in the large dining room about to partake of Beef Wellington. The evening's feast was rapidly progressing. By contrast, Mrs. Perkins was becoming eerily quiescent. I had little time to waste, so I decided to take an unilateral action.

I installed Mrs. Perkins in a wheelchair and rolled her along to the loading bay inside the clinic's front entrance and effected the brakes on her chair. At the valet's station, I found the keys for an ambulance parked nearby the garage. I hopped into the driving seat, backed the vehicle to the front doors where I opened the rear door of the vehicle and hauled out the mobile gurney.

I walked back to the wheelchair, unlocked the brakes and wheeled Mrs. Perkins out of the building and repositioned her from the wheelchair to the gurney. It was an easy operation to insert my patient into the gurney and place it into the back of the ambulance. I secured the gurney, folded the wheelchair and pushed it into the vehicle alongside the gurney. I closed the ambulance door. I ran back inside the clinic to tell the receptionist I was taking the patient to the ER of the local hospital. I said I would complete her de-admission paperwork when I returned.

Alone, with Mrs. Perkins securely tethered in the gurney at the back of the ambulance, I drove the patient to my barn where I carefully transitioned her to the one empty accommodation in the clutch, making sure in the process of doing so that she was comfortable and had everything she required at hand. It was a chore to lift her from the gurney to her new resting place without a wheelchair, but she clearly appeared to appreciate what I was doing for her. I took the gurney back to the ambulance, stowed it and drove back to the clinic. It had been a very risky thing, but the patient was now where she belonged. At the time it did not matter who had botched the exercise.

I was furious to discover the perpetrator who had deposited Mrs. Parkins in my institution without my prior authorization, but I did not have time for sleuthing now.

By the time I was back at the clinic and had joined my colleagues in the refectory, dinner was over and dessert had begun. My alert signal indicated Miss Maras was on the move. I decided to do the paperwork on Mrs. Perkins' case at once back in my office.

Not ten minutes later, I knew I had been snookered. My barn alarms went haywire. As I flipped through the Perkins papers as fast as possible, I had visions of the middle-aged patient wreaking havoc at the barn. Meanwhile, when I checked the *other* alarm monitoring Miss Maras, I discovered she was jogging directly toward the barn to join the party happening there. In the distance, I distinctly heard the sounds of several police and rescue vehicles converging on the woods.

When three hours later I reached the piers at the marina, I parked my vehicle in the back of the lot and covered it with the expandable soft cloth to keep it hidden as long as possible. I walked along the pier to the place where my boat, the *Lamia*, was berthed.

Once on board, I required a quarter of an hour to get her underway. I was in the channel using my twin engines with my running lights on, counting off buoys as I approached the end of the channel and turned south toward the Caribbean. I unfurled my sails and cut my engines. Consulting my cell phone's mobile apps, I noticed all my barn alerts had failed. That meant *someone* had terminated my clutch and found and disabled the device Ralph had planted in Miss Maras's overcoat. It did not occur to me right away that Perkins and Maras had been working in tandem, but later the coincidence seemed compelling.

I did not have to puzzle out *what* had happened. Instead, I had to make my way to Port-au-Prince, Haiti, by the best possible route. There I would make shift with assets I had sequestered there and start again to build a fresh clutch, as I always had done before. Things might have turned out otherwise if Miss Maras had decided to use her wooden darts on me at the clinic. Why she had not done so was a mystery to me.

"Dr. Alilović, you have a visitor in the reception area. Dr. Alilović to the reception area, please!"

I was in the middle of a procedure in the ER of St. Damien's Pediatric Hospital of Port-au-Prince, the least offensive medical hell-hole in Haiti. Nothing meant more to me than saving this young boy's life, so I ignored the loudspeaker. The fact that someone who knew my name had found me did not make me feel warm and fuzzy. Anyway, having absconded from the Clymer-Holster Clinic the prior spring, I did not expect the police dragnet to extend to my current venue.

I did not make haste but finished the operation, cleaned up, changed out of my scrubs and made my way to the reception area. Alicia, the receptionist, told me a tall, powerfully built juju man had come looking for me. He had left his *carte de visite*, which confirmed the fact: 'M. François Gérard Deladier, Juju Man,' it read. An address and phone number were included. I thanked Alicia and pocketed the visitor's card.

I do not like to leave unfinished business, especially when a juju man is involved. So I put on my darkest shades and my floppy jungle hat and went to the address on the juju man's card, which happened to be a grave in the Grand Cemetery in the center of the city, not far from the apartment complex where I was living. On a bench near the grave in question, a huge black man was casting bones with three friends. He did not look up right away when I asked where I might find someone named Monsieur François Gérard Deladier, Juju Man.

His three companions drifted away, leaving me facing him alone. The juju man was laughing.

"Monsieur Deladier, I am sorry I missed you at the Children's Hospital. I was in the middle of performing a critical operation at the time."

"I know what you were doing, Doctor. I am glad you had the good sense to continue fixing the boy's problem. None of my magic had done him any good. Let's hope your medicine works better than mine."

"Why did you come to see me today?"

"I knew you were coming to Haiti long ago. I know why you are here. The trouble is, Haiti is a very crowded place, spiritually speaking. Many specialists are chasing too few customers and too many people are looking for them to make trouble."

I looked him in the eyes. "Are you offering me protection?"

"I don't think you need my kind of protection. Let's say I am offering you a chance to know what you seek to know but can't know without me."

I nodded. "What do I seek to know?"

"For one thing, you seek to know what actually happened when you left your former place of employment."

"What will it cost me to make this discovery?"

"It will not be expensive in monetary terms. If you want to know this, come at midnight to the grave on my card. Bring a bottle of whisky, nothing else. I will cause you to see. Then you can decide what that knowledge is worth and pay me accordingly."

I nodded and turned away. The juju man went back to casting bones. As I was about to cross the street, I looked back and noticed he had disappeared.

For me, Haiti is an old stomping ground since the beginning of New World settlements. It is always changing in respect to its spiritual hierarchies and forever the same as well as to the number of top dogs amongst its holy practitioners. I have no problem employing people connected to the dark spiritual side as they are often the only guides who can clarify ambiguous conundrums."

That midnight, I was at the appointed grave with an unopened bottle of whisky. The juju man materialized, accepted my gift and opened the bottle. He sprinkled some of the brown liquid on the grave and drank some too. He began to moan and sat on the grave with his back to its headstone. His eyes rolled up under his upper lids, and he began speaking in a mix of French and English.

Near the clinic was a barn full of vampires. Property you owned but did not own. One great vampire wanted to kill your clutch. Another great vampire needed to steal your clutch. In the end, the killer used sharp wooden stakes to kill, and the thief in frustration killed the killer with sharp wooden stakes. Now thirteen who were not alive are dead. You who are not alive remain.

There is more. I can deliver a clutch to you here in Port-au-Prince. It is governed by the great vampire who wanted to steal your clutch but failed. If you do not kill this vampire, you will be killed by him. What do you choose to do?

The juju man handed me the bottle and gestured for me to drink. I did this and felt imbued with the spirit. I also had questions.

"Where is this vampire's clutch, where is he, and how can he be killed?"

"His clutch is in this very graveyard in a mausoleum under the name of Mobius. That is also where the vampire lives. You know the answer to your last question."

"Will you help me destroy this clutch and this vampire?"

"For gold, yes. My three friends and I will help you."

"Why are you willing to do this for me?"

"The ones we shall kill have done irreparable harm to me and mine. I do this for revenge."

"What will you require to do this work?"

"Thirty-one sharp wooden stakes. The time is the next midnight. Drink nothing and eat nothing until then or we shall surely fail and die."

I handed the whisky bottle back to the juju man. He laughed and screwed down the top. Tucking the bottle under his shirt, he said, "When the work is done, we shall drink the remainder. I will now show you the exterior of the mausoleum."

The route to our goal was a maze, but I thought I

could remember the way through it. When we arrived, I studied the exterior of the structure wondering how a clutch of thirty-one beings could fit within such a diminutive edifice of thirty cubic feet. The juju man disappeared, and I spent hours returning to the point where I had entered the maze.

The following morning, I went shopping for thirty-one sharp stakes. I bought them from a voodoo priest who sold all manner of spiritual artifacts. From another such vendor, I bought an additional four stakes for no reasons other than a hunch.

I was hungry, but I did not feed. I was thirsty, but I did not drink.

I spent the day working at St. Damien's Pediatric Hospital where I extracted a bee's stinger from the white of the eye of a four-year-old girl and successfully discussed the merit of not amputating a boy's little arm at the elbow but to save the whole arm instead.

By the time I left the hospital, I was extremely hungry. I wondered when I might be able to feast again. I felt the tell-tale delirium beginning: without blood, madness would ensue.

That night was a religious festival. The entirety of Haiti was embroiled in rituals of every kind, particularly voodoo. I did not want to be late for my appointment, so I set out early after work from my office to thread the maze in the cemetery.

I arrived at the Mobius Mausoleum at eleven PM. I was not surprised to find the area deserted. I did not want to become the target of potential assailants, so I ducked behind the structure and waited where lush, tall vegetation completely sheltered me.

The juju man and his three cronies showed up half and hour later.

The head man briefed the others about what they

26

were to do: "At the stroke of midnight, we shall go into the crypt and use the stakes our pigeon gives us to kill all the vampires. Be careful to kill all thirty-one of them. When we are certain they are all dead, we will emerge from the mausoleum and kill Dr. Alilović too. Then we shall be supreme among the dead."

When I overheard the juju man's words from my hiding place, a chill ran down my spine. I was glad I had bought the four additional stakes. My only question was whether I could kill all four of those men before one of them killed me. I backed silently through the foliage around the rear of the mausoleum so it would appear I had walked from the opposite direction and had no no idea what the juju man had said to his cohorts.

At five minutes before midnight, I approached the front of the building where the others stood. I distributed the thirty-one sharp stakes to the four co-conspirators, making sure the four additional stakes I held were not visible.

At the stroke of midnight, the four piled into the crypt to instigate their killing. I remained outside, waiting for them to finish their murderous work and emerge. When they emerged after forty-four minutes, the juju man was first, and I drove a stake forcefully, with both my hands, into his heart. Each of the other three followed and met the same fate—a wooden stake through the heart. I then rushed into the crypt; my lit lighter helped me find thirty-one berths wherein stakes had impaled the now-ashen hearts of skeletons of the former demons who drank the blood of the populace.

I emerged from the mausoleum satisfied my mission had been accomplished. By then my four murder victims had turned into ashes and bones, which convinced me they were, indeed, vampires, and not humans.

I made my way back out of the maze of the cemetery at three o'clock. The all-night's festivities had abated somewhat, but fireworks were still exploding near and far in the air. The uniformed authorities were moving through the city to create a semblance of order out of chaos. They were particularly numerous in the old colonial section, which included the graveyard I had just left. I slipped into my apartment, glad to have missed the next phase of the police action.

The next morning, I followed my usual routine as if nothing untoward had happened. At the Children's Hospital, I carried a full load in ER. I expected at any time the police would come to question me, and I was afraid. But I had no need to worry. What had happened in the graveyard had no clear definition in legal terms. The authorities apparently did not care what happened to vampires and the undead. Though I was not clear about every detail, I felt confident I had broken no laws. Things might have been different if the juju man and his gang had been humans. As it was, those four just disappeared. I only hoped they stayed dead as I had heard stories of vampires being resurrected. Those four deserved death for their perfidy.

I waited two weeks before returning to the Mobius Mausoleum. Little had changed. Rain had washed the ashes from the bones of the four dead outside the building. Inside, the situation had not been altered one iota. I did not want or need help to refurbish the mausoleum so I could use it for my own clutch. I had purposefully brought two hundred heavy plastic bags with me for the bones and ashes into which I put the bones and ashes of the thirty-one skeletons. I doubled-up the bags so they would not break. I then transported the residue by a huge night refuse vehicle. which accommodated all those filled up bags, not to mention the weight of each one, net of my thirty-five sharp stakes, to the dumpsters outside the city incinerator.

The interior of the mausoleum cleaned up nicely, yielding thirty-one berths for new inhabitants. The ivy and other vegetation around the exterior, once cleared of the deceased human detritus, luxuriated.

I oiled the hinges of the door, and the Mobius Mausoleum was once again the finest venue for a clutch in Haiti. This augured well as, during the clean-up, I had begun a binge of feasting to make up for the starvation and hallucination I had endured. It only took three months to collect thirty residents for my new venue, the thirty-first berth being reserved exclusively for me.

I never leave odds and ends behind me. It was only when the Port-au-Prince clutch was a going concern I became determined to return to the Clymer-Holster Clinic in Virginia and pick up the pieces of my broken enterprise there. I arrived at the marina one year after the date of my departure aboard the *Lamia* to reclaim my automobile, which still lay under its tarpaulin. The car's battery needed a jump-start from a tow truck, and I filled its gas tank on my way back to the clinic.

I entered the front door like a returning hero, not a prodigal son. I assumed the load my associates had carried in my absence and settled down to work.

Two weeks later, I visited the refurbished barn in the woods and found residue similar to what I found in the Mobius Mausoleum. All eleven of my cohorts had been slain in their berths by sharp wooden stakes driven through their hearts. In addition, two female figures lay dead from the same cause on the floor. I used the same methods to clear out the detritus as I had in Haiti, only here I dumped the remains in trash receptacles scattered throughout the adjoining counties. I retained the thirteen sharp stakes for further use.

A month later, the eleven empty berths were full again. The twelfth and thirteenth were a spare and my own. Business was humming for me at the clinic. I was sorting through my patients for the ideal recruit for the twelfth berth. When I thought everything was returning to normal again, I reminded myself I now had the Haitian clutch as well as the clinic hutch of my own to manage. Then too, I was not satisfied by the juju man's accounting of what had happened at the barn. His story had been too pat. For safety's sake I began to take back-bearings to rethink everything. Once nearly bitten, I did not want to be bitten again. That would be stupid, and I like to think I am not an imbecile.

So, what had really happened to upset my equilibrium? Who would have benefitted from stopping my operation in its tracks? I thought the two women who had separately converged to effect my demise were the pivotal point at which to start searching for answers. Someone had sent them against me with explicit instructions to terminate my operations and kill me. Those shadowy figures had different ways of conducting their business. The actor behind Miss Maras was sophisticated and subtle but lacked conviction, else I would be dead with a stake through my heart. The other entity behind deploying Mrs. Perkins was both sloppy and insouciant, but she managed to go right to the heart of the matter, literally.

Day and night, I wrestled with the known facts. Then I began to speculate: *The two women who visited my clinic were single and of those Perkins was a widow. I could never trace either woman via the normal channels. Medical records contained no references to family or other emergency contacts. It was as if they came from nowhere, and their disappearances were unremarked since the fatal incident at my barn. The wound marks on the neck of Mrs. Perkins linger in my memory as a desecration of technique and practice.*

I thought evidence of other victims with neck indications like those of Mrs. Perkins might lead me to the clutch presided upon by the mastermind behind her. I began to frequent bars and dives where women of her character sought out men. In fact, my search pattern was little different from the one I used to find food. If ours had been a territorial struggle, I figured I might intercept a competitor and trace him or her to ground.

My other line of approach was via real estate. On weekends, I drove all byways within seventy miles of my clinic, looking for a venerable yet hidden abode which could contain a clutch. After I had searched the woody areas, I coasted through the avenues that paralleled the beach. It occurred to me a seedy, old hotel would be perfect because it would be practically invisible to the upscale clients of grand hotels. Further, the beach at night offered food of high quality and numerous paths for flight in the event of discovery.

I admit my search served my personal needs as well as my concern to eliminate the competition, amongst whom would be vampires like me. It also allowed me to expand my horizons for business for the clinic.

My opportunity presented itself in the same form as it had on the prior occasion. One Friday evening a widow, having the same profile as Mrs. Perkins, attempted to check in to the Clymer-Holster Clinic. For Mrs. Clara Sampson, the presentation was identical, including the neck lesions.

I refused to admit the woman to my clinic but drove her at once in the ambulance to the nearest hospital emergency room. She struggled to escape, but I orchestrated her evaluation by the duty ER physician. I remained only as long as it took for the hospital to garner her emergency contact data.

I waited outside the hospital that night figuring Mrs. Sampson would escape and return to her clutch. When she emerged before four AM and took flight, I followed, unobserved by her. She wandered along the beach avenue closest to the ocean and slipped into a decrepit four-room hotel sandwiched between two luxury spas. I waited long enough for her to clear out of the lobby. I then entered the flop house and booked a room for the next four hours under the name 'John Smith.' The hostess had the tell-tale marks on her neck, so I knew I had hit the spot by recognizing the imposter for what she was.

As daylight dawned, I had surveyed the four floors of the building and, on the top floor I found a renovated area with twenty-five coffins. I resolved to leave the premises and return the next morning before dawn with twenty-six sharp wooden stakes. The additional stake was for the hotel's receptionist. I admit I did not calculate what might happen between the time I left and the time I planned to return to the hotel.

Mrs. Sampson persistently reappeared at the clinic early that evening, insisting she could not be cured at the hospital. She was unruly and threatened to become violent. I went through the motions of admitting her to the clinic as an in-patient and gave her a sedative. I secreted a sharp wooden stake in the pocket of my white examination coat.

When night fell, I checked her out of the clinic and transferred her to the ambulance strapped to a gurney. I did not drive her to the barn where my clutch was sequestered but to a clearing in the woods. There I drove the stake through her heart and watched her turn to dust. Leaving the woman's remains in place, I walked back to the clinic.

I had plenty of time to fill my leather satchel with twenty-five stakes. I no longer required twenty-six as Mrs. Sampson's heart held one. I had no trouble checking John Smith into the four-storey hotel on the avenue across from the beach. It took me thirty-four minutes to fulfil my task of eliminating the vampires driving my stakes into the residents on the fourth floor.

The receptionist was sleeping behind her desk when I came down the stairs. She was snoring, with her head back and her green kerchief almost hiding the teeth marks on her neck. I drove the final stake through her heart and left the hotel immediately.

I returned to my clinic in time to make my morning rounds. I immersed myself in my work to forget what had happened in the hotel. I did, however, marvel that thirteen of my victims had been males and thirteen females. I did not anticipate anyone tracking my movements from the hotel to the clinic, and it seemed I had gotten clear of the beach before anything amiss was discovered.

For three weeks following my last visit to the hotel, nothing appeared in the local newspapers about the extermination of a clutch of vampires at the beach. I did not return to the hotel to retrieve my stakes as I did not want to take the risk of exposure. I was not at that stage assured that I had terminated all the vampires in the vicinity. I remained vigilant, looking for signs of another active clutch besides my own.

I do not want to give the impression I was solely focused on the activities surrounding the clinic. At the same time as I was eradicating the competitive clutch in the beach hotel, I was remotely monitoring the situation at the Mobius Mausoleum in Port-au-Prince, Haiti. I had engaged a horticultural firm to take care of the greenery around the crypt and inform me of any attempts to vandalize my property. The net effect was to draw unwarranted attention to a mausoleum everyone seemed to have forgotten.

I had disposed of the ashes and bones of my victims well enough not to have caused a stir among the local police. The current clutch I had established was getting along as well as I might have expected. The juju man and his three henchmen had vanished without repercussions or police reports according to my informant in Haiti. I received my monthly bills for gardening work, but otherwise everything was quiet on that front. I wondered why the former proprietor of the mausoleum had not gone ballistic at the damage or at least taken revenge for the installation of a new clutch by an 'outsider' like me. I use quotation marks around the word outsider as Jure Grande Alilović, under a varieties of pseudonyms, has been a distinguished resident of Haiti for hundreds of years.

My clutches in Virginia and Port-au-Prince are only two of many scores of facilities throughout the world. Why, I even have a clutch on the southern shore of Lake Superior in Minnesota, USA, and another near Lake Baikal in the city of Irkutsk. I favor the world's largest bodies of fresh water as they are among the most likely places to foster future growth.

I have a good memory, but even I have trouble keeping up with my holdings. I am, of course, wary of signs that vampire hunters are about to raid or reveal my operations. Only a few such predators are worth my trouble, and I found it tiresome that one of the best vampire bounty hunters should drop by the clinic to see me for a professional chat.

There was no mistaking the fifty-five-year-old Viking Sigurd Nilsson for anything other than the vampire killer she was. Over six feet tall, with long blond hair reaching to the small of her back, she wore black leather garments and a necklace with a brooch featuring a woman warrior driving a stake through the heart of a classic vampire.

We had become acquainted over the last twenty years, and the topic of our intermittent conversation had never varied. She was on the trail of vampires; it was her chosen quest of genocide that enlivened her and gave her joy.

"Dr. Alilović, I am glad to find you in. I am in Virginia on one of my missions. Do you have a few minutes to spare to answer my questions about blood pathologies?"

"Sigurd, it is good to see you again after a dozen or so years. How is your hunting progressing?"

"If you have a private room, I will gladly fill you in on my latest. Perhaps that will repay you for the expert knowledge I require from you today."

I followed procedure by requiring Sigurd to divest herself of all weapons before we entered the consultation room. I was chilled by the number of sharp stakes she had been carrying. Additionally, she carried two pistols with silver bullets."

I served us both hot tea with biscuits as we sat across from each other in leather armchairs by the picture window. "It is your nickel, my Viking lass." I could not help but admire her poise and grace of movement.

She was acutely aware of her effect on virile men, so she smiled at my explicit admiration. "I am tracking an enduring vampire with clutches worldwide,' she explained. 'My people have deployed the latest technologies by providing me high-grade information and intelligence on a daily basis. Since we last spoke, my financial backers have pooled an amount in tens of billions of dollars. I am held accountable to the penny, but if I demonstrate the need, there is no limit to the resources I can devote to a project."

"Congratulations, but what can I do for you that your money will not buy a thousand times over?"

She munched on a biscuit and sipped her tea before she answered. "You have unparalleled knowledge of human blood. You have unmatchable intelligence about vampire behavior. And you don't treat me in a patronizing fashion. Further, you have never made a serious pass at me or abused me sexually or in any other way. You know I cannot buy what you have, but I can be grateful for what you give me." She was toying with her brooch, aware of its lethal significance.

"Fair enough, Sigurd. What do you need from me today?"

"I require your consultation on three things, in no particular order. First, until recently I was tracking a vampire woman named Perkins, Inez, a widow. She had the strangest bite marks on her neck I have ever seen. She was rumored to have been seeing medical help in this vicinity. I need to know whether you saw her."

"A woman with that name did try to check into this clinic, but I was alarmed by her condition and felt she might be better off at a local hospital ER. So off she went, and she never returned to this clinic."

"What alarmed you about her condition?"

"She was delirious and foaming at the mouth. Her bite marks were typical vampire marks, only they were infected in a non-traditional way."

"How non-traditional?"

"When a vampire bites, he or she makes minimal incisions with razor-sharp canine teeth. The intent is to provide food for the vampire without jeopardizing the source. The vampire's saliva serves to heal the wound and not leave a suppurating wound for infection to take hold."

"Hm. Do you think she may have been given

36

vampire-like wounds by someone who was not a vampire?"

"The thought occurred to me."

"There is no record of Perkins anywhere within a hundred miles. Did you keep a record of her emergency contacts?"

"As she never was admitted to the clinic, there was no need. So we don't have any of the usual information about the patient. Maybe the hospital ER would have such data. Surely, she had health insurance."

Sigurd was shaking her head. She pushed onward: "Second, my intelligence team has indications of a major liquidation effort at a vampire clutch in Virginia Beach."

"I have read nothing about that in the newspapers. Does your team know where the clutch was located? Or who did the liquidating?"

"Unfortunately, no and no."

"I thought you might have a best guess as to where such an event might have taken place—if indeed it ever happened."

She had leaned forward in her chair and now held her brooch in both hands.

I knitted my brows and said, "You have two choices in Virginia Beach—the woods and the beach. The latter has a mix of old buildings that might house a clutch. Perhaps an old hotel? Certainly not one of the big, modern, luxury ones."

We sat puzzling over the possibilities separately. "You had a third requirement?"

Sigurd was hesitant. She took a deep breath and continued, "Yes, I did. One of my protégées, a single woman named Maras, Letitia. She checked into this clinic and became your patient. She was on the trail of Inez Perkins for me, but her last message indicated she was leaving the clinic to follow a new lead. Then she was silent. She just vanished from the face of the earth. I am convinced she was killed. I am compelled to find out what happened to the girl." Her eyes were welling up, and I thought she might weep.

"That young woman did stay here under my personal care, and she was progressing well before, as you say, she simply disappeared. Naturally, I was unaware of Miss Maras's covert mission for you. If she was killed, I am so very sorry for your loss."

Sigurd burst into tears and wept for a long time copiously. I gave her a box of tissues but I could not console her. When she eventually stopped crying, we rose to our feet. I let her pick up her weapons, and then I showed her to the door.

"Goodbye, Sigurd. Don't be a stranger. Drop by more often in the future. Whenever you like."

"Thank you, Dr. Alilović. As always, you have been most helpful. The next time I need to infiltrate your clinic, I will brief you about the mission in advance."

The Viking woman warrior turned and strode off to her vehicle. I suspected she would delve into every aspect of Mrs. Perkins' and Miss Maras's disappearances. I knew she would do the same exhaustive search for clutches I had done myself. I also guessed she would stop searching for the clutches when she found the devastated one at the beach hotel.

Sigurd was a natural retributive force, and I loved her for her thoroughness and dedication. I only hoped she would not find my barn in the woods. We had never waged war against each other, and I disliked intensely the thought of fleeing from her as an alternative to fighting her.

I decided to avoid the barn for the foreseeable future and toyed with the idea of traveling to another of my clutch venues until such time as the Viking lass had done her worst.

Contrariwise, I saw a distinct advantage to Sigurd wreaking her brand of mayhem in Virginia Beach: if there was another rival clutch in the vicinity, she would likely find and destroy it. That would save me the time and trouble of performing another intensive search myself and eliminating the clutches I discovered in the process. It would also obviate my need for additional sharp stakes in the near term. However, I did make a mental note to replenish my stock of weapons in case I should require them.

I envisoned Sigurd might return to update me on her progress. Four weeks later, she did exactly that. We went into the special conference room again, and over tea she told me she had found the remnants of the devastated clutch in the four-storey hotel across from the beach. She had called her forensics experts to the scene to remove every shred of 'evidence.'

"They might find something significant,' she said, 'but I do not think they will find anything as telling as the sharp stakes the perpetrator used as weapons. Each stake will be examined at the 'nano' level, but we may never find the man or woman we are looking for. I am convinced the stakes are among the finest in the world, and that alone might tell us something. But we shall see."

I asked, "Will you keep searching nearby in Virginia, or do you have other fish to fry?"

"I believe I have found the big cache. Maybe it will give me another step in the right direction, but maybe not. I want the biggest prize—and so do my financial backers."

"What, may I ask, is the biggest prize?"

The Viking giantess smiled. "I am seeking not any *grand* vampire or any *great* vampire, but the firstborn vampire from whom all the rest have descended."

"Wow! Indeed, that sounds like a life-long quest."

"Dr. Alilović, you know it is more than a single-life-long quest. I dream of a time when *all* vampires have been slain. My friend, just as the human blood pool has become contaminated, so all vampires have been corrupted. Take, for example, the condition of Mrs. Inez Perkins. Such carelessness should seem to a medical man like you a heinous crime. Well, does it?"

"Yes, Sigurd, it does. Today's vampires, by that measure, seem to have no pride. If I had so little pride in my work as a doctor, my patients would all become terminal."

"I am glad we have a common understanding. I am now going far away to examine another clutch exhibiting such criminal insouciance. Keep your eyes open. There's no telling when another specimen such as Mrs. Perkins will drop on your doorstep. When that happens, I hope you will be in touch with me. Here is a card containing my contact data. Keep it private and use it well."

She handed me her special card. I examined it and slid it into my wallet. The interview was concluded. I made sure she had collected her various weapons before I escorted her out of the clinic's front door.

After her automobile disappeared, I was tempted to run straight to the barn to make certain that everything remained as I had disposed of it. But I did not—in case the area was under surveillance. Instead, I carried out my normal duties for the next five weeks when I received her postcard from a small town in northern Minnesota.

That same evening, I went to the barn and found it unmolested. I reasoned I was safe, for now.

I then went trolling at the beach where I discovered that the police tape was still wrapped around the four-storey hotel where the vampire clutch had been found. The building was apparently empty with a 'CONDEMNED' sign on the front doors. I tried to imagine what might be done with the property once the original building had been demolished.

I continued walking past the hotel on the opposite side of the street. The warm beach breeze lured me down to the sand where the waves played incessantly and the seagulls cried throughout the day.

I was suddenly ravenously hungry. A well-built young man in a scant swimming suit waved at me from his position in the water and smiled as if he knew me. It was too far for me to inspect the man's neck; I waved and smiled back but moved on without making advances. I needed the exercise, and I liked to make the first move in any case, no matter how hungry for blood I was.

Gathering wool in the balmy salt air, I mused on Sigurd's stated quest to find the Firstborn. It was like looking for the fabled 'missing link' between *homo sapiens* and the most intelligent apes, or looking for evidence of *Zep Tepi*, the 'First Things.' What harm could come from that kind of search? The problem— and the harm—I knew from experience, was the unintended consequence of the search itself.

The Viking woman warrior did not care to think of such consequences. Would she accept the truth that in order to know the firstborn vampire she must first become what she was hunting and a blood relative of all vampires? At this stage, that would be heretical to her secular religion and antithetical to her quest.

Foremost among Sigurd's motives was revenge. In a flash, I had seen she genuinely loved the young woman named Letitia Maras. Did the arch vampire-slayer realize her beloved was herself a vampire? I suppose not. I still wonder how the action sorted everyone out in my barn. No matter. It was unknowable.

Concerning Sigurd's successful work to eliminate my clutch in the log cabin near Lake Superior: nothing I could have done would have changed the outcome. Besides, no records linked the cabin to me by any of my identities. My thousands of other clutches are similarly disposed, and collectively guarantee the survival of vampires generally. Whether called *firstborn*, *grand* or *great*, we, the oldest and most powerful vampires, have earned our bragging rights by merely surviving against the odds.

For the sake of completeness, I did not discount the case of Mrs. Clara Sampson, whose name never arose during my discussions with Sigurd. I found her contact data at the ER of the local medical facility in Virginia Beach. The data were largely false, but a reference in them to a nursing home in Chesapeake, Virginia, seemed worth checking out. I bided my time before I made enquiries, but it came as no surprise that I would check on a patient whom I had referred to ER. Though the name Clara Sampson was not in their records, one Mrs. Edith Sampson was listed amongst long-term care patients at the home.

I visited Mrs. Sampson to discover how her daughter Clara was faring as she had almost become my patient.

"Dr. Alilović, I have not seen my daughter Clara since she left here to consult your practice weeks ago. I'm surprised and a little alarmed you could not accept her as your patient. You came so highly recommended by my own personal physician, Dr. Phillip Roberts."

"Do you know why Dr. Roberts made his referral to me?"

"You will have to ask him that question," she replied.

I garnered the contact information about Roberts from a card he had left with Mrs. Sampson. The man

42

stemmed from a long line of physicians and morticians who practiced in Chesapeake. Before I visited him, I checked his background thoroughly. In the Land Registry records, I discovered Roberts' extensive holdings of farms throughout the Virginia Tidewater. A quick survey of his farms yielded sightings of at least half a dozen barns, three of which looked promising as habitations for clutches.

I had no trouble locating Dr. Roberts at his home practice. I reached him by telephone and received a warm reception. The man did not hesitate to set an appointment for that afternoon.

"Sorry to bother you, but as I told you on the phone, I wanted to close a peripheral case on a missing person named Clara Sampson."

"Of course, Clara! Normally, I would have called you before I made my referral, but my patient wanted to meet you straightaway about her condition."

"By the time she arrived at my clinic, she needed emergency attention, so I delivered her to the nearest ER. After that, I lost track of her. Did she reconnect with you?"

"No. Once she left here, I assumed she would be helped by you or someone else in our profession."

"Can you tell me why you made the referral?"

"Clara appeared to be suffering from an infection centering on punctuation marks on her neck. As your specialty is hematology, I thought you might help her sort things out."

"As you formerly thought I might help Mrs. Inez Perkins?"

"Why, yes. But I understand she, too, has disappeared."

My eyes swept Dr. Roberts' office until I found a Bell jar full of sharp wooden stakes.

"What I deduced was a recent history of malpractice

43

in both patients. If you were not involved, will you tell me who their personal physician was?"

"I take umbrage at the word *malpractice*. I come from a long line of distinguished physicians and . . ."

"And morticians. Yes, I have read your bio. I think you can give me a detailed account of your diagnoses and treatments for both your former patients."

Dr. Roberts sighed and turned to examine his stake collection. I did not hesitate to drive my own stake through the man's heart. My action had an immediate effect as the doctor's corpse disintegrated into dust on the floor.

I harvested his desk calendar as well as his files on Clara, Inez and Sigurd. I also picked up his stake collection of well over 25 before I left his office, closing the door behind me. In the passage to the front door, I noticed a painting of one of his renovated barns, the same edifice I would have selected if I had been in his shoes.

As I drove away from Dr. Roberts' practice, I made a few mental computations. I did not hesitate to do detailed planning but drove to the renovated barn in the painting, which was a prominent property visible from the highway. There I rushed inside to find an orderly arrangement of twenty-five slumbering vampires. Applying the doctor's stakes, I pierced each of them through the heart. I might have burned the entire barn to the ground, but what was the use? Nothing was going to improve the man's defective practice at this stage. The unmistakable signs of infections indicated the sloppy work and slovenly attitudes that cannot be reversed by good intentions.

I drove back to my clinic, satisfied I had finally found and destroyed my local competitor and his clutch. My only surprise was finding Sigurd Nilsson's file among the others on my desk. A brief perusal of her file convinced me she too had become a vampire. Clearly, Roberts had used her and his other two patients to destroy me.

Though I did not originally consider it advisable to go to Lake Superior, I now knew it was essential to do so. I had already made arrangements for my colleagues to cover my workload at the clinic, so I rented a sea plane to fly to the southern shore of the greatest of lakes to meet Sigurd, without announcing myself beforehand, in the middle of her operation against my secret clutch in Minnesota.

When I arrived late in the mid-afternoon after flying a rental sea plane all the way from the Tidewater, I noticed the building containing my clutch was thus-far unmolested. Once on land, I discovered Sigurd and her team were staying at the main hotel while they planned their operation. She appeared to be delighted to see me when I found her at the hotel's bar.

"Dr. Alilović, it is so good to see you again."

"Hi, Sigurd. I'm glad I found you. I regret to announce that your personal physician, Dr. Phillip Roberts, has died suddenly. His death, obviously, means the end of a long medical tradition of his family. Please accept my deepest condolences for your loss."

"I need no condolences. Dr. Roberts and I were not close."

"You did share two of his patients, Clara and Inez, in your work."

"That we did, but our relationship was purely professional. Do you know I was one of his patients too?" Sigurd's left eyebrow raised slightly when she said this.

"I read your file. And it makes sense, given your life's mission to discover and extirpate vampires wherever they may be."

"How do you figure that?"

45

"The only way to get close to your prey is to become one of them. It was inevitable for you to join their ranks. I am sure you knew that."

"Why don't we get out of this bar and enjoy walking along the shore? It is brisk, but beautiful this afternoon."

So there I walked beside a beautiful blue-eyed Viking blonde vampire as the huge waves from the lake hit the shore with a continual crashing din.

"Do you know the legends of the corpses in this lake?" I asked her.

"There are many such cadavers. Perhaps, you are thinking of the fact that dead bodies in this lake do not decompose."

"Divers have found specimen corpses a hundred years old and more perfectly preserved, roiling around forever in the frigid depths."

"Is that your sea plane bobbing out there on the waves?"

"Temporarily, yes. I rented it in the Tidewater. I will be flying back soon.

"Now that you know about me, where does that leave us?"

"Sigurd, face it. You have become what you most desired to hunt. You are a living contradiction, a figure caught in the middle between two states. Whatever you choose to do about that, I confess I love you just as you are."

She laughed. "Surely you jest, my friend. Whether you are, as I suspect, a vampire, or not, you are a mortal threat to me. Now that you know my secret, I must be a mortal threat to you. Somehow I have a hard time thinking of you and me wrestling to drive stakes into each other. Worse, I find the prospect of either or both of us going up in smoke abhorrent in the extreme."

"Of course, a grand problem requires a grand

solution, Sigurd, if only we are willing to live with the consequences."

She smiled faintly. "You are not factoring my Viking pride into your equation."

Unfortunately, I knew better than she about her pride. "Decisions that are not easy should not be forced."

"Will you go diving with me this evening?"

"I suppose I could find a wetsuit and full diving gear."

"I have everything we need at the hotel."

She knew I could plunge my stake into her heart at any time, and I knew she could do the same to me likewise. Yet we had a date to go diving beneath the surface of the greatest repository of fresh water in North America. Two vampires risking everything together.

Consequently, we went diving in the place where the bodies played endlessly in the water. We descended with our spotlights and observed a kaleidoscope of wonders, whole crews of sunken vessels and unlucky divers. We were both wary as we swam, keeping our distance from each other while having our sharp stakes ready in case of an attack by the other.

As we explored the silent depths, we came across an ancient sturgeon twenty feet long, a pair of star-crossed human lovers tangled in each other's arms forever, a deceased terrorist whose unmistakable face we had seen blazoned on the international news broadcasts. The man's facial contours continued menacing all-comers as the motions of the water kept him down; suddenly, and appearing from out of nowhere we were attacked by a team of five men and five women with knives. I smiled at their innocence: knives held no danger for vampire initiates.

I turned the attackers' own knives against their own

47

hoses and masks. All ten were lost, and I saw Sigurd was then poised to use her stakes on me though we were friends.

I shrugged and beckoned at the Viking with one hand as with the other I held my stake. It was a dilemma I presented to her, and she knew it. After a few moments, she sheathed her stake, and I sheathed mine. We returned to the surface and swam through the waves to shore. It was nearly midnight, and the cloudy skies threatened rain. Having swum hard to defeat our common enemies, we made the beach gasping for air.

After taking off our flippers and our tanks and full-face masks, we walked to the hotel to take a hot shower outdoors before we returned to our separate rooms, changed and had a late meal.

Sigured's blue eyes were sparkling after our underwater exercise; she laughed as she admitted she was glad about her decision.

I wrinkled my brows. "Tell me what you have decided."

"I am going to abandon my mission to eradicate a clutch of vampires in this town as my team has perished in the lake." I was flabbergasted by her admission that the attackers were her team members.

"Will you join me in my enterprise?" I had no idea what I was offering her at the time.

"Whatever it is, yes, I shall." So she was willing to risk an association with me in any case.

We touched wine glasses as a sign of our agreement and promised we would postulate the details of our pact in the morning.

The next day we visited my clutch. We discovered Sigurd's people had destroyed all my vampires before the team decided to dive and kill us underwater. Sigurd was as surprised as I was at the outcome.

"You had a good team, Sigurd. They did a thorough

job. I expect if they had known what they were dealing with in us, they would have killed us both. But they did not."

As quickly as we could, we tidied up our affairs and planned our departure. We commandeered a dingy and took our belongings to the sea plane. We took off in the early evening and spent most of our flight to Virginia talking about our future. We realized we were essentially loners who must go our separate ways. By the time we landed, we had made a pact of friendship going forward. There was no sense in our feuding. There were victims enough for the two of us in the world.

As I turned in the rental sea plane to the charter company, Sigurd made her own arrangements to fly to Rwanda to pursue her lifelong dream to see the headwaters of the Nile River. I resolved to go back to my clinical practice in Virginia Beach until I had a chance to think things through on my own.

Sigurd and I confirmed our agreement to keep in touch and, generally, to keep out of each other's way. We shed no tears at our parting.

I have given some thought to rebuilding my clutch on Lake Superior. As I mentioned earlier, locating near the largest bodies of fresh water might increase the odds of survival—if such an increase were needed. But Lake Titicaca in South America might serve just as well, and I still have my clutch in Irkutsk.

THE HAMADRYAD

Myron Banks, the trusty lab assistant and janitor for Nano Robotics LLC, walked behind the bioengineering facility into the swampy woods to dispose of the latest failed experiment in creating synthetic life capable of reproduction. He had no idea what might happen when the five liters of organic substances melded with the specimens he had dumped in the forest over the last fifteen years. His job was to distance the residue from the latest lab work 'somewhere where the sun did not shine.' End of story.

But tonight, it was not the end, only the beginning. Banks wore hip boots that crunched through the decaying debris of rotting wood in the process of advanced decomposition. The putrid stench of the swamp made his head reel though he was enchanted, as always, by the phosphorescent glow of the rotting vegetation brewing in the black water.

He chuckled as he thought about the company's youthful technicians' excitement about their xenobots. As he poured the contents of his container into the vivid soup, he was unable to witness the change the liquid made in the dark. Anyway, it was, like any organic chemical process, exceedingly slow, but in the forest, it no longer required human Ph.D. scientists to do its languid work.

Banks was not a superstitious man, but tonight he thought he heard the cry of a young woman in distress in the swamp. He called back asking whether the female in question required his assistance. He was affronted when his offer was met with a derisive laugh. Angered by the rebuff, he turned and walked back to the lab where he washed his container before making his usual notation in the log book. He checked the temperatures of the continuing experiments in progress. He thought no more about the disposal of the waste. Like all the other such janitorial tasks, the dumping was merely a checkmark item on a schedule, nothing more.

The forest that surrounded the Nano Robotics xenobio lab was thick with wood and wet with decaying detritus. Some felt it was in the beginning stages of becoming a petrified forest. The Ph.D. scientists joked they might be on the wrong end of their experiment. Perhaps, they jested, they should be studying the process of decay in preference to alternative modes of regeneration and reproduction. Dr. Charles Lamont, the Chief Science Officer, never joked about his work in this way. The others sensed he was so narrowly focused he might just win the Nobel Prize for his breakthrough experiments. He had no sense of humor that any of his colleagues understood. He was exceedingly brilliant, a confirmed bachelor and a workaholic.

Today he was taking Myron Banks to task for taking the wrong batch of liquid into the forest for disposal the previous night.

"With all due respect, Doctor,' Banks explained, 'the container I emptied was the same I always empty on Friday nights. I had no instructions to empty another. If I have erred, it will have been the first time in the last fifteen years."

"It seems we will have to chalk up your error to a 'spilled milk' state of affairs. We cannot recover from it, so we shall have to leave it 'as done.' In future, though, please consult me before you release our compounds into the forest. If you don't, we are likely to face the wrath of the EPA and other agencies. The lab will be shut down then, and you will no longer have a workplace. More importantly, the compounds in your dumping place might interact with each other with no predictable consequences."

51

The janitor grimaced and went back to his duties. Dr. Lamont might have called the EPA to report the matter of the dumping, but he had another important xenobot experiment to conduct, and he did not want to waste his time complying with trivial government regulations.

The forest surrounding the xeno lab was perpetually inundated by the Chickahominy River, which also fed the fresh water reservoirs of numerous adjacent cities, villages and towns. It was also a hunters' and trappers' paradise harboring prize animals such as black bears, whitetail deer, beavers and muskrats.

Nick Bounder, a sixteen-year-old woodsman, helped his mother make a living by selling the wild game and furs he harvested on the black market. Like his now-deceased father, he was successful precisely because he did *not* follow the rules.

Bounder kept clear of the small businesses that pock-marked the borders of the swamp though he detested the dumping those businesses did in his wilderness. The pollution spoiled his own business. It also caused changes in the environment itself. The boy felt closely bonded to the wilderness, and he hated anyone who encroached on its ancient natural rights. He knew places in the swamp where no other men had yet penetrated—limpid pools rich with fish and ancient stands of bamboo and papyrus. He would cut bamboo shoots with his knife and use beeswax to fashion them into the pipes of Pan. He had also experimented making paper with papyrus as the ancient Egyptians did.

Nick was an autodidact and an original in every sense of the word. He was a fool who did not consider anything but the surface meanings of things. He was also a trailblazer who ventured where no man had dared go before.

Two weeks after Myron Banks had dumped his waste into the forest, Nick Bounder sat on a rotting tree stump to play his Pan pipes after checking his traps. He played his rustic music and watched the insects swarm in the starlight and admired the iridescent glow on the wet fallen trees and the fetid water. He heard, as often before, a hidden maiden singing harmoniously to his melody.

Nick concluded his piping, but today the female voice continued to sing. He had nowhere in particular to go, so he listened carefully to the woman's words. Hers was a sad song of a woman whose life depended on a tree that had fallen. She had thought all was lost until one day her tree was given a drink of healthy liquid that reversed its natural process of decay. Now she felt young again and looked forward to the growth of green shoots stemming from crannies in the fallen tree. As a woodsman, Nick's heart beat in sympathy with her song. He found in the marshes the green shoots she had sung about, and he rejoiced in her theme of life springing from death. This reversed his expectations and gave him hope for other things that sprung from unpromising origins to surprise and delight.

In making his nocturnal rounds from that time forward, Nick stopped to pipe by the fallen tree where he had heard the young woman's voice. Like a Druid, she sang interminably, though never once repeating the stanzas of her lyrics. He could not see her, but her voice projected into his mind her image as if she were standing before him naked with her long, golden hair covering her breasts and spilling down to her knees. He often held out his hand so she might take it, but she was shy and reluctant to make contact.

The more frequently they met, the more real she became, though her reality was a mesmerizing fluorescence rather than one of flesh.

Visiting her dwelling place each day, Nick saw her transform from a faint shadow into a multicolored neon buxom lass. He thought her transformation might have been occasioned by the green shoots from her tree. So, he composed a tune about that transmogrification and, from the way she smiled when he played it, the ditty seemed to please her well.

The third time she heard him pipe his tune, she sang a song she had composed to suit it. The song captured his unspoken notions with uncanny exactitude. Seeing it pleased him, she came close and touched his pipes with her delicate fingers. At that point, he realized she was not just a figment but alive.

From that first contact forward, Nick's piping improved as did his facility to compose. The young woman sang increasingly joyous spells, and the frogs' mating cries were her chorus. The tree's shoots sprang higher and higher between his visits. The sheen of iridescence now extended in all directions as if he were witnessing the swamp's general resurrection.

Meanwhile, the experimentation at the xeno lab continued. Dr. Lamont redoubled his efforts to perfect his recipe for xenobots, but each new failure led to new waste, which was disposed of by the janitor in the same way as before.

Inevitably, Myron Banks returned to the place where Nick Bounder and his forest creature made their music. Not believing what he was hearing, Banks crept up close enough to listen to the singing and piping. By starlight, he noticed how lush and green the new shoots were growing. With a wild surmise, he intuited what must be happening as these transformations were connected to his company's xenobot experiments.

When Nick departed after his latest performance, Myron stepped forward to dump his organic residue. The female creature smiled at him in gratitude for

54

replenishing her tree's nutrient liquids. Rather than pressing forward, the janitor fled back to the lab to inform Dr. Lamont what he had seen.

The doctor did not wait a moment to brood upon the news, but importuned the janitor to take him immediately to the location where he had witnessed the seeming miracle of a young forest woman embedded in a tree.

The glow of the woman's aura had not diminished when the two men arrived at the base of the tree; the female was still luxuriating where she had stood before on the rotting stump where she had been standing. After he recovered from this stunning vision, the doctor tried to communicate with the young woman, but she either did not hear him or distrusted him. She remained silent. The doctor took notes on what he saw, and he resolved to return to the place the next night to talk with the piping woodsman whom Banks had described.

Back in the lab, Dr. Charles Lamont meticulously reviewed his records to discover what among his developments might have caused the lush growth deep in the forest where light seldom shone on the universal vegetable decay. His interest in the young woman was a secondary matter for him as he saw no apparent connection of her to his work. The janitor, however, had fallen in love with the image of the beautiful female. As the doctor was preoccupied with his experiments, the menial conspired how he might woo the young forest woman as his wife.

The next night, four figures met deep in the forest: the doctor, his janitor, the woodsman and the forest maiden. The woodsman was vexed to have others intrude on his 'personal' preserve. The maiden refused to sing while the janitor was entirely fixated on her naked form. The scientist was firing a hundred questions in quick succession at each of the others without getting any answers.

The three men were about to come to blows when the young woman raised her hands and asked them to remain quiet while she sang a song. The exception she made was for the woodsman to use his pipes.

The pipes made music as if by their own accord, and the young woman's singing was different from anything the woodsman had yet heard. The song told of the birth of a young woman in a tree to which she was bound until the day it died.

The tree did die. It fell and began its slow decay of two hundred years. She remained next to the tree, expecting to perish as well. Magical substances were spilled into the surrounding waters, and new green shoots formed, betokening a subsequent cycle of life— both for the tree and for herself. She sang that she was grateful for the renewal she felt in her body. She had never expected a reversal of the process of decay.

The scientist asked the maiden how the fragmenting process of decay had been reversed, but the maiden had no notion. She did know everything changed when the janitor brought his liquids to her tree. This angered the woodsman, who might have vented spleen about the desecration of nature with pollutants, if the maiden had not counseled calm.

"As my tree revived from the nutrients out of the materials dumped in the water, I felt those same active particles coursing through my veins to give me energy and hope."

The scientist pulled two petri dishes from his lab coat and collected samples from the standing water. He raced back to his lab with the janitor in his wake. After the commotion, the maiden asked the woodsman whether he was game to make music. Of course, he was game! The two piped and sang until dawn. Then the woodsman went home leaving the woman to her thoughts.

Dr. Charles Lamont found in his two samples what he had been looking for. By an 'accident of nature,' his experiments had been successfully completed. He awarded the janitor an enormous bonus and stock options in his company after apologizing profusely for having berated him earlier. Once they learned the details, Lamont's colleagues thought their lead scientist was now a shoo-in for a Nobel Prize.

The scientist was subsequently so busy at the lab, he neglected returning to the dark center of the forest where the maiden dwelled. In the meantime, she had prevailed upon the woodsman to transplant her tree's green shoots to another place deeper in the forest where they would not be disturbed by meddlesome outsiders. The woodsman was happy to oblige her.

The janitor continued to dump residue from his company's experiments in the same place as he always had done, but now the maiden was gone and the woodsman had apparently changed his routine. Though Myron Banks was now a man of means on account of his bonus and his stock options, he had not won the love of his life.

The woodsman, by contrast, remained relatively poor, but he loved hunting and trapping; he looked forward to making music with his maiden even though she must remain with the shoots from her tree, deep in the swampy forest forever.

THE CARRIER

The mutations evolved so fast the global medical community could not keep pace, but what began as a manageable serial of viruses overnight transformed into nightmare variants with transmissibility and infection rates beyond anything experienced in human history.

Politicians had attempted to quell popular unrest, but the deaths-per-day in the big cities staggered the imaginations of the masses. So the political pundits were hunted down and—literally—crucified while the media encouraged hysteria by broadcasting the horrors of disease and retribution in equal measure.

Sherill McCabe had been lucky. Her family had perished as a result of the scourge—not just her nuclear family and both pairs of grandparents but her first cousins and second cousins wherever they lived elsewhere in the country. The disease did not discriminate by age, gender, neighborhood or income.

Through the social media Sherill's friends reported their physical conditions and exhibited selfies until, exhausted from their attempts to fight the plague, they published the effects of hemorrhagic fever in their bloody faces and jaundiced, bloodshot eyes. Some died of drowning in their own phlegm; others, despairing, resorted to suicide.

Daily, Sherill waited for the inevitable symptoms of her own demise, but, so far, no sign of the disease had entered her system. Others accused her of having a biological advantage over the rest, some miraculous and rare immunity that set her apart and preserved her. The religious envied and resented her purity of life and believed this to be the 'reason' for her special station among humans.

Before she decided to leave her office forever and work exclusively from home, Sherill's co-workers had mourned with her as the families, theirs and hers, succumbed. Only a few of her die-hard co-workers remained in the former office complex for a time—till the last of those texted her that their business headquarters had closed on account of attrition. Her company was going to fail. There was no way to stop its irreversible decline.

The funds in Sherill's bank accounts were dwindling, but she was increasingly worried the food and goods delivery people would stop providing their services. The delivery people continued to wear protective masks—which was a national imperative—but they joked about having early symptoms.

Then, without notice, their replacements came to deliver; she lost count of the changeovers in staff as they had sickened and died. Sherill thought she might eventually die of starvation rather than disease. She expected an imminent announcement in the media that famine and scarcity had shut down grocery and paper goods retailers just as the pharmacies and banks had closed on account of medical riots and bank runs, respectively.

Sherill used her automobile sparingly. With gas running at over twenty dollars a gallon, she had tanked up early and only turned over her engine occasionally to keep her car's battery running. Besides, where could she drive? The virus was rampant.

The city of Gilbert was collecting the dead in handcarts to save fuel. Hospitals were becoming makeshift morgues; existing morgues acquired new mobile annexes with no possibility of climate control like air conditioning. The stench of decomposing bodies competed with the fumes of crematoria working day and night, and redolent smells of excrement emanated from the city's overflowing sewers.

Municipal infrastructure no longer provided running water. Toilets would no longer flush. Distilled and purified water was only available in two-gallon increments, twice a week. Before water ceased flowing from taps, it had become illegal to water lawns or take showers. Sherill had filled her garage with bottled water by the gallon, and paper goods like facial tissues, toilet paper and towels. She had not used her washer/dryer for two months.

The young woman had trouble remembering the last time she had taken a hot bath or washed her hair. Given that electric power was only available two hours a day, she had become accustomed to life without artificial lights and only two hours of news reporting on the TV.

Outside on the streets, she heard the sound of trash compacters, which had been commandeered by the authorities to collect dead bodies instead of trash. She looked out her front window where two masked workers were using a bobcat to transfer six bodies wrapped loosely in sheets to the gaping, open mouth at the rear of the enormous, deep-green vehicle. She shuddered as the compacter lowered and scooped the human flesh as the bodies were automatically pressed into the capacious containment area.

When two of her neighbors importuned the driver to take a few additional corpses, he claimed his vehicle's capacity had been reached. He shouted out to them that he would return the day after tomorrow and drove off as her neighbors shook their fists and hurled imprecations at him. Sherill's mind wrestled to factor how long it would take those additional dead bodies to decompose during the ensuing forty-eight hours' wait.

That same night, an enormous black hearse came down the road outside Sherill's dwelling in utter darkness to pick up the same additional bodies across the street. The funeral vehicle was notoriously expensive for ordinary citizens—well over five-hundred dollars in cash—and it was full to overflowing its capacity of ten bodies when it arrived. Rumor had it the midnight hearse drove to dump its harvest either in the open desert or in the reservoir.

The police could not be everywhere at once, and catching looters was their priority. Reported thefts were off the chart, and numbers of murders were trending down significantly with fewer slain as there were simply not as many people available to be killed as before the plague.

This plague was prime time for outlaws. Sherill had witnessed a roving band of brigands foraging in her neighborhood in the interval before the community watch had been formed. Only her neighbors with guns and abundant supplies of ammo survived that night of pillage. She had shot four of the men and two of the women in one particular outlaw band. She had allowed them to bash in her door so she could gun them down *inside* her home where she had the legal right to shoot intruders dead. The policewoman who investigated the incident afterwards congratulated Sherill on her presence of mind and advised her to buy more ammunition since the police no longer answered 911 calls for routine burglaries.

Animal control had similarly broken down throughout the city. Former pets of deceased citizens roamed the streets alongside herds of javelinas and feral cats. Coyotes hunted in the culverts in the early morning, and huge barn owns thrived on account of the ready food. Early mornings also saw new waves of illegal immigrants sweeping through the city. Coming north from Mexico through the porous border, desperate families were trying to connect to those of their relatives who remained alive in America while

61

simultaneously attempting vainly to avoid catching the dread disease.

Walking through her neighborhood at dawn with her gun in her hand, Sherill witnessed an ecosystem where people devoured dogs, cats and coyotes, which they roasted over open fires in the public parks. She watched as families bathed themselves in standing water from the Monsoon's run-off. One man used his rifle to shoot a mallard duck which had been unlucky enough to land in that same water. A pack of wild dogs raced into the water to eat the slain duck before the hunter could taste his fallen prey.

Sherill enjoyed the quiet that had descended on the city. Trains continued to clatter through the neighborhoods, as always; vehicular traffic had almost entirely been eliminated and bus services had been severely curtailed.

The former coming-and-going of landscaping service crews had ceased entirely. As she walked through her neighborhood, she noticed the lawns were brown. The only flowers that thrived without water were red bougainvillea and orange manzanilla.

In the curb areas in front of nearly every dwelling was a body wrapped in a white sheet for pickup. Some bodies had lain there neglected for over a week. They seem to have bloated by natural decomposition.

In the park were the six crosses where the city officials had been crucified because they were corrupt and had taken bribes to make exceptions for wealthy citizens. The bodies remained there nailed to the rude wood as examples to others, but no elections had been held to replace those who had been executed by the people. Crows sat on the cross-beams and cawed at each other. Flies and wasps swarmed to feast on the offal.

Sherill wished to be home before the parade began in

order to avoid the huge numbers of people. Today was the Day of the Dead, a celebration of life and death, appropriate in this time of widespread, indiscriminate death. She wondered how many celebrants would participate in this plague year. Warnings about the dangers of personal contact had been published by the same people whose faces smiled in rictus fashion from the crosses in the park. No one knew who to believe anymore. Few cared anyway.

She heard the approaching beating of drums and the sounds of a large, raucous crowd. She walked quickly in the direction of her home, but the sounds seemed to be nearing her location fast. She broke into a run and managed to get into her house and lock the door behind her before the parade marched by. It was led by two figures: a male and a female wearing death masks and walking on impossibly high stilts.

She watched the crowd pass right by her front window while an occasional celebrant leered at her from the street. The colorfully masked and costumed people had appropriated sheeted bodies from alongside their path. The parade had now become a funeral cortège of sorts, the bodies in sheets being raised and lowered by those who supported them. Stray dogs and cats followed the procession around the corner. Soon Sherill could no longer hear the celebrants singing. Then the drumbeats ceased.

Sherill realized she was still carrying her weapon. She put the pistol back in its holster and hung her shoulder rig on the peg back of the front door. In the street boat-tailed starlings pecked at oiled papers that had held food eaten by a reveler. A gray feral cat eyed the birds hungrily. A white pigeon lay dead under the pin oak tree. On the top of the lamp post across the street perched a watchful, giant barn owl.

A tear ran down Sherill's cheek. She supposed she

was involuntarily weeping over the death of the white pigeon. She tore two precious sheets of paper towel from her roll and went to where the pigeon lay. Gently, she lifted the creature with the towels and verified it was genuinely dead. She took the tiny corpse through her house to the back yard and laid it on a cinder block by the kumquat tree. She resolved to bury the creature in the sand lot after dark.

Back inside the house, she answered the bell to find a delivery of two gallons of water. The masked delivery person was a newbie, who seemed pleased to see a customer wearing a mask. "I am glad you are home. The parade people are used to pilfering like the porch pirates."

Sherill said, "Thank you for your concern. How is your health holding up?"

"So far, so good. The girl I replaced died horribly at Dignity."

"She was lucky to have been admitted there."

"I want to die at home, not in an institution."

"Here's hoping you won't die at all!"

"No offense intended, Ma'am, but we all check out of the Earth Hotel sometime, I suppose."

Sherill nodded. She brought the water inside and closed the door. Then she debated whether to shave her legs. Usually, the process consumed half a gallon of water. She opted to wash her face and clean her privates instead. Though she still felt shaggy, she also felt clean where it counted, and the whole, albeit sparse, ablutions had required one fourth of a gallon of water instead of the half gallon the shave would have taken. She took her temperature and used the medical swab to confirm she did not have symptoms of the viral disease. She was pleased to have lived through another day.

The lights blinked and then came on. Sherill knew

she had just under two hours of electric power to catch the evening news on the TV and make her dinner of tuna fish from the can, with crackers.

A new story recounted the repurposing of cruise liners as ferries for the terminally ill on the Gulf of California. Patients in sheets were shown bundled into rooms and cabins below decks where the carnival atmosphere was in full display, with sound effects like those of a casino. Why there would be such a happy atmosphere when such critically ill patients were on board, Sherill could not determine. The cruise line staff were advertised as fully-licensed medical personnel. As a courtesy, burial at sea was an option for passengers at a modest additional cost.

Sherill marveled at how people were willing to spend their money. She made a mental note that one such repurposed cruise ship was departing at dawn from a pier at the northernmost point in the Gulf of California. The advertisement promised the cruise would keep the passenger's mind off the troubled present while providing every luxury imaginable. The inevitable electric power loss made the lights flicker. Sherill lighted a red candle and put her tuna-fish can into the garbage, having wiped out the empty contents first with a tissue.

Her doorbell *rang. Standing* in the vestibule was the young woman who had delivered her water earlier.

"You already delivered the water."

"That was my drop-off. I am back for a pick-up. I have been instructed to escort you to your cruise."

"My cruise? Surely there must be a mistake."

The young delivery woman read the order from her computer. "There is no mistake."

Sherill felt faint and collapsed on the vestibule floor. She awakened three hours later at the dock where the cruise ship was about to cast off its line and depart.

Two orderlies in nursing costumes conveyed her aboard and arranged her in a bed in a cabin which was reserved for privileged customers below decks. They fiddled with an IV, the contents of which were dripping into her left arm.

Over the carnival sounds and the low hum of human voices, Sherill heard the captain welcome everyone aboard. She felt the juddering of the ship and knew the vessel was now underway. She might have protested to the authorities, but the drugs were clearly in control of her volition now. The face of her delivery woman, she realized, was the same as that of the woman on stilts in the parade.

THE GREAT RIFT'S REVENGE

"The beauty of this place is beyond words," Ophelia said as she broke into the meadow by the lake. On all sides of her panoramic view, giant trees loomed, and behind them mountains rose, forming a natural basin of luxuriating green foliage and water.

"We can admire the scenery after we've placed the birds and other sensors," Lloyd said, working fast to open their tent. Ophelia situated the cages and sensors around the tent in spiral fashion, taking care each bird was lively and every sensor was active.

The previous party had done everything by the book—and still all the scientists perished mysteriously. Dr. Lloyd Stickler was a perfectionist, determined to accomplish his objectives and ensure that they both returned alive.

They worked in the high clearing for an hour-and-a-half, then checked out the monitor that fused sensor data in a near-real-time display in the tent. They tested their array of sensors by activating the alarms in sequence. The innermost spiral arm contained forty caged birds, one for each cage, which were lively in their new surroundings. Satisfied they had a protective shield of sensors, Dr. Ophelia Sanders unpacked her unmanned air surveillance system, otherwise referred to as UAS.

The first wide area sensing of the lake area was conducted via the UAS. The fixed wing aircraft made a circuit of the meadow before it surveyed the lake perimeter. Finally, it flew high enough above the mountains to spot key areas of interest such as the cave where the Marburg virus had been found and the remains of the deserted native village on the far lakeshore. Not two years prior, the entire population of that plot of hutments had been wiped out in a single

67

night by causes yet unknown. By the time Ophelia brought her mini UAS in for a landing, she and her colleague knew little more than they could determine from satellite resources.

"The bird activated none of its onboard sensors during its flight. I will perform analysis of the filtered residue. In fifteen minutes, we should know if trace elements are present."

Lloyd replied, "I am particularly interested in the most minute indications of sodium dioxide or hydrogen sulfide. Either or both of those killer gases would account for the deaths at the village."

"Yes, but where is the source from which they might have emanated?"

He gestured expansively to the pellucid lake where flocks of water birds stood in mockery of the scientist's theory. There was no mining or oil exploration within fifty miles of their camp's location. Both investigators were playing hunches about the mystery of the deaths as they had nothing whatsoever to go on.

"Lloyd, on the off chance we do get a positive reading in the middle of the night, pray what is our plan to avoid asphyxiation?"

"We have been over this before, but it bears repeating. We have our masks to filter the air while we file our reports. We also have our oxygen supplies which will each last for four hours. If we take the eastward path out of the basin, we should be able to keep ahead of any rising gases."

"Maybe we could do a practice evacuation tomorrow morning?"

"We could do that as a precaution."

"Meanwhile, to get through this first night, we will need more than bug repellant to keep the insects from devouring us."

Lloyd smiled and tossed Ophelia a bottle of strong

repellant before he broke open the mosquito netting they had used in their Amazon and Congo River expeditions.

"I wish we were doing more than relying on our hunches," she said as she liberally applied the noxious-smelling juice to her exposed skin. When she had covered herself, she walked down to the lakeshore to watch the sunset. Lloyd came up beside her with a coil of netting as protective covering, which he offered to share.

They stood under the thin-gauge netting and watched the water birds across the lake while the humming and buzzing of angry insects indicated the pests were trying vainly to penetrate their makeshift shield. The sun set below the level of the mountains making visibility difficult thereafter. Still, Lloyd was troubled by what was happening to the larger birds.

"Ophelia, how fast can you fly the UAS to the other side of the lake?"

The young woman raced back to the tent, then rejoined Lloyd to get her apparatus into the air. She flew the UAS remotely to the place where the birds were apparently disturbed. Not a hundred yards from her target, the airborne sensors sang about the presence of the worst case scenario of threat gases.

Lloyd did not have to tell her to pull on her mask as he did the same. "We are going to have that drill you mentioned starting right now, only this is not a drill, it's for real."

Ophelia steered her UAS back to the meadow at maximum speed. Within fifteen minutes of the vehicle's arrival, she had performed her analysis on the residue it had collected. She and Lloyd worked out their report. He included the time of their intended exodus from the camp site and sent the analysis to their sponsor's headquarters unit with their intention to climb the mountain to a pre-determined rendezvous point where any arriving rescue craft would pick them up.

The spiral of sensors was now sounding alarms. Ophelia made a quick survey of the caged birds to find them dying off fast. "It is time to leave for the mountain rendezvous." The time was now two AM.

Lloyd had already gathered their oxygen supplies and torches which he had placed in his backpack. The two scientists found the path to the east and steadily followed its incline. His mind was whirling with calculations. He reeled off his thoughts out loud as he wondered whether they had enough time to outrun the enveloping gases.

"Ophelia, let me know if you need to slow our speed of advance. Everything depends on our remaining ahead of the rising tide of poisonous gases. The way they affected the birds across the lake—and then the birds around our camp—indicates a fast effluent from some source, probably at the bottom of the lake."

"I am doing fine so far, thank you. We can be satisfied we found the source of the mysterious deaths, and we sent our results back to headquarters. Our mission is accomplished."

"Yes, but we have many more missions to accomplish before we expire—at least I do."

"Do you want to push a little harder, Lloyd?"

"We had better continue a sustainable pace. Our hand-held sensors have not yet been triggered by the gases. Even if a sea of gases is being released, the natural basin is enormous. I estimate it will take two hours to fill a quarter of the volume. We are lucky the lethal gases are heavier than the ambient air."

"My hand-held sensor is blinking red on-and-off for both gases now."

"So is mine. Keep right on as our masks will take care

70

of the gases until they signal their capacity has been reached. Then we have to shift to oxygen."

"No one told me science was an Olympic sport."

"Hold on to that thought. You will have a story to tell your grandchildren if we get out of this alive. I think I hear a helicopter. Do you hear it too?"

"It must be heading for the rendezvous point. At least something is going right."

"Yes, let's keep positive. The path looks clear ahead, but the grade is steeper. If you can continue climbing at the same speed of advance, we should be able to keep ahead of the tide."

"When I think of all those lake birds dying—and all our caged birds too!"

"Don't get absorbed in things we can no longer control. Keep right behind me, and let me know if you need to rest."

Ophelia laughed. "Just keep going, cowboy! If I feel like fainting, I will let you know. By the way, my hand-held sensor is now reading solid red."

"Mine is red too. We must keep climbing!"

"And the grade is increasing as we go."

"I cannot figure why the gases are filling the cavity so fast. It hardly matters. Do you feel faint? We can switch to oxygen if you like."

Ophelia said, "I am getting faint. Let's switch now."

The scientists switched to their oxygen and flung their masks to the side of the path. They consequently had compressed oxygen from their masks that took them to the landing area where their rescue helicopter was waiting for them. The intrepid pair were greeted by the rescue team, who helped them strap into their seats on board before the rotorcraft took off.

The rescue chief said, "The whole basin is filling with poisonous gases right to the brim. The helicopter took off in time to avoid a catastrophe."

"We are grateful," said Lloyd. "It will take some study to get to the bottom of the leak, but it seems nature has a mind of her own. It was as if we were known quantities, and she was bent on vengeance."

Ophelia said, "We were lucky to have avoided her wrath. If my guess is correct, a fissure running straight down the Great Valley Rift stands ready to dissuade human interference with her primal will. I will never forget her alluring beauty, but it is matched by her anger."

"We solved one mystery, only to unfold another," Lloyd said.

Ophelia said, "I have seen and experienced enough of this mystery. Once the gases have subsided, we can capture our samples and do our final evaluation, something our predecessors did not have the opportunity to do."

HALLOWEEN ON THE ESCHER HIGHWAY

Blind Hansel Hedwig in cerements strapped himself into his place in the electric car at the time when trick-or-treating was supposed to start. He had been informed that the vehicle was programmed to stop at all the usual dwellings in his vicinity, then to swing out on the Escher Highway and finally return when the evening's festivities had ended.

Lacking vision and being blind from birth, Hansel compensated by making the most of his other senses, particularly smell and hearing. In his perpetual darkened world, he knew the route through his immediate neighborhood by heart. As he progressed, he addressed treat-givers by name through the rolled up window of the vehicle and thanked them profusely for their kindnesses. Many offered him compliments on his clever costume. He did not share his secret.

When he walked alone, the other children often said hello and wished him good luck before they ran off laughing in twos and threes into the night.

With his sack full of candies, Hansel felt his car pull into the on-ramp of the Escher Highway, a first-ever experience for him. The SatNav system in the car announced out loud the routes the car was taking. He was not sure what to expect but was game for surprises, though not a little apprehensive about his ride and his itinerary as he was wary of untested automation. The vehicle rose on the winding pavement stage by stage until he heard human voices. The car seemed to be moving at times through trees whose bare branches brushed against both its sides simultaneously. He smelled the spores within the rising dust and sensed the muffled sounds of people dancing, playing and singing randomly. Suddenly, the vehicle stopped where the pavement ran out, and the windows rolled down automatically.

A female figure approached his window from the right side.

"You are new to these parts. I'm Vilia. May I join you in your car?"

Hansel answered, "Climb right in, but I warn you this contraption has a mind of its own. I would not know how to catch up if it took off without me. My name is Hansel."

As the young woman opened the door and sat down next to him in the passenger seat, he smelled rosemary and lavender as from a tussie-mussie or nosegay. She touched his arm gently with her left hand, and her companions outside the car began to sing the familiar 'Vilja Song' from the Hungarian composer Franz Lehár's operetta *The Merry Widow*. This song was one of Hansel's favorites, and the young woman rendered it in the sweetest voice.

When the song ended, Vilja, as that was the young woman's name, told Hansel what she saw around them as a kindness since he was blind: "Your car has stopped just short of a deep ravine in a blasted landscape visible by the light of the full, pink moon. Human figures dressed as you are surround your car on all sides carrying fardels of bound twigs and baskets of loose earth. Where they are bearing their harvests is unclear, but they are moving along the highway in various directions without complaint."

"Can you tell me where the Escher Highway is from here?" Hansel asked.

She laughed. "Wherever your car can go *is* the Escher Highway. That's for certain. Lower down through the bare trees I see what might be infinite extensions of the highway, also lined with people with sacks over their shoulders. Do you want to get out of your car and play with me?"

74

Hansel shook his head. "I had better not do that. I have no idea when the car will decide to move on. I don't want to be left behind. If I could see, I might not be afraid to venture forth regardless of the vehicle's intention."

Vilja said, "If I were you and I could *not* see, I would remain in the car too. Well, then, I must be going. On this propitious night, I have little time remaining to explore my surroundings. I'm glad we met out here even though our time together was brief."

"Thank you for spending some of your precious time with me. I rarely get out alone with autonomous transportation. But being with you has been worth the whole journey."

Hansel tried to reach her with his hand but kept missing her. She eventually had to guide his hand to her face. Thereupon his fingers traced bones and her long hair which was tied with a ribbon. One of his fingers ran along the raw edge of her jaw.

"Pardon me, but I am trying to visualize your face."

"Take as long as you like with your braille." She kept her face steady while he explored with his sensitive hands. When he nodded to signify he was ready, she said, "I must be going now, Hansel. Goodbye."

"Goodbye, Vilja. Meeting you out here has fulfilled one of my fondest dreams."

"Now that we have met, Hansel, we can meet again whenever you fancy."

She slammed the car door as she descended from it; the vehicle started again and backed up, retracing its remembered motions. The roadside figures resumed singing their 'Vilja Song,' and Hansel shed a tear when he heard Vilja's voice pick up the melody.

Hansel could not afterwards describe the lengthy route between the hillside on the Escher Highway to his neighborhood—fortunately, his vehicle seemed to know the way well enough. Outside his dwelling again, the door of the auto opened without his assistance.

Hansel released his seatbelt and got out of the car. He tested his footing and stalked up the walkway lined with tall, closely-planted yew trees to a low stone building with a sunken iron door. The door squealed on its rusty hinges as he pushed it open. The air inside the enclosure felt damp and cold and smelled musty.

As he lay on the stone slab in the center of the room with his ancestors ranged around him in their compartments, he fondled the chocolates in his Halloween sack and enjoyed the earworm endlessly repeating 'Vilja's Song' in his mind.

As he tried to drift off to sleep, Hansel reviewed his night's ride through his neighborhood and the Escher Highway. He realized he had had Vilja's eyes to thank for his experience of the latter. He tried to envisage what the young woman looked like in the evening. Her momentary touch was helpful in convincing him of her reality, as much as bone on bone could be.

Far off outside emerged the sounds of the midnight chimes of the village church. On the twelfth chime, Vilja came through the door to lie next to him. He sensed her presence though he could not see her. The only light was emanating from the shining moon; he could not see it but she could, at least until the iron door closed itself after she had found her way to a place on the slab by his side.

"So, your car did bring you back here safely. And I found you because you were thinking of me."

"Yes, you came here too, all the way from wherever we met—in time before the midnight hour was chimed! I am so glad."

Hansel, having heard the iron door creak and slam, felt safe in the knowledge that they were now in pitch blackness.

"Now we are *both* blind, Vilja. Yet when I hear you sing your song, I am able to see."

Pleased by this, she moaned softly with pleasure and began singing 'Vilja's Song' once again.

Hansel relaxed as their folded bones joined together, hers over his. He imagined infinite figures with their fardels returning late at night through the poisonous yew trees. His fertile mind conjured the features of costumed children who, having toted sacks of chocolates, now lay in their beds sleeping peacefully, though not yet ready for their last, long sleep.

He confessed, "For a while, I despaired I would ever escape from the Escher Highway. I thought I might become trapped, as in a labyrinth. Then you appeared out of nowhere."

Vilja stopped singing to consider this idea. She said, "Have you ever thought the Escher maze might have been devised as a catalyst for transformation?"

"I have often thought my blindness is such a catalyst, as it was for John Milton, the English epic poet. Poetry is a cross-over art inviting introspection."

Vilja said, "I was released from bondage by your finding me in the woods. I followed you here, a consequence you must have anticipated."

For a long period, the two contemplated their discoveries, bones on bones.

"You were more hoped for than foreseen. Now here we lie hopeless, and neither of us can see."

"Still, our bones form a testamentary ossuary. Eons hence we shall be discovered by perfect strangers, you in your peasant's garments, I in my waxed cerements," Hansel declared.

He heard the deathly silence as she pondered this. "You knew me from my song. How shall I know you?"

"Think of me as a mute, inglorious Milton, a would-be poet who perished before he ever penned a line. As there is no way back to rectify my lot, let me spend my eternal days paying tribute to your charms."

She laughed. "My story is contained entirely within the operetta's libretto."

"Where does the poet write of our midnight tryst on All Hallows' Eve? Where does he factor a star-crossed young man and his ideal young woman coming together to piece together his words, her features and her music not as ephemerides but durable, lasting until the very end of time?"

"Where shall we begin?"

"Where else should we begin but where we first met—on the Escher Highway?"

She laughed, and he could feel her bones shake. "We hardly know each other."

Now he too was laughing. "Such intimacy as ours cuts through society's niceties. From the moment my index finger touched your jaw, I knew we would grow together somehow. As I was drawn to you, so you were drawn to me. On this dissection stone, we are surrounded by the Hedwig clan. I shall be introducing you to each of my ancestors. You shall do me the honor of acquainting me with your forebears too."

"This talk of mutual history mocks our fragile knowledge of each other. Gyre not from a moment to all time lest I become bewildered and lost. Focus on hard details, not fuzzy generalities. As we need to, let us tether our consensual poem to the operetta, from which I stem."

"Yet for me, you have always been mortal in the way of no other mortal and immortal because of your insubstantiality."

Vilja laughed. "Rummage through my bones and feel for yourself how much such substance is worth in a moldy crypt. I am a peasant. As such I value love in the sturdy concrete, not in the dreamy ephemeral. Further,

I want to own, not owe my soul. If a poem should celebrate me, I need to find the truth of me in it. Do you understand me?"

"We have each other at cross-purposes, I think. Being blind, we are beginning to see where we diverge. A collection of bones, we still have individual conceptions. Tell me, how many other crypts of dreamers have you visited whilst floating the prospect of enduring love?"

"Countless. On the highway, the cars bring me men of all flavors, and some women too. In their eternal habitats, we mix and sort as we have done, Hansel. Try as I might, I cannot escape who I am, not should I break from that which I truly am."

Hansel nodded. He felt the young woman arranging her bones while standing free of the stone tablet on which they were lying.

"So, poet, I hope you understand why I cannot stay with you. My search continues for the companion who sees and accepts me as I am. I do not believe in accepting relationships with the hope of reformation on either side. I cannot prohibit you from writing whatever version of me is entrenched in your mind. Please help me open the iron door and close it behind me after I have left. The next time you venture outside, you shall find your vehicle has vanished. It will take me back to the Escher Highway where I shall continue my quest which is to know myself in death as I never did in life."

Hansel got up, then worked the door and in so doing felt her touch his jaw. He envisioned but not did not see her march down the line of yew trees to the car. He barely heard it drive off. Then, he shut the door and lay back down on the slab alone. Sleep fell like a curtain, and the earworm was finally silenced.

EXISTENTIAL PUMPKIN

Tween Randolph applied the knife so well that the skin came off in corkscrews, leaving a translucent shell of horror. His chubby hands hollowed the insides by pulling out orange skeins and seeds creating space for one thick red candle. He tested his new Jack-o'-lantern on his sister, whose objection was the jagged row of teeth which he soon removed with a soon-bloodied hammer. On the front porch he placed it to smile with others, a scary crew, himself included, on the one evening evil ruled the earth.

The trick-or-treaters clamored for candy, but Randolph glowed and smiled saying, "I choose trick for you." Nonplussed, the little ones wracked their brains and scrawled charcoal figures on the sidewalk or spread cobwebs along the outside sills of windows. Word got out and focused everyone on mischief. Black cats yowled and raised their backs and tails. Witches landed, brandishing their brooms. People piled deadly nightshade berries, black and red.

In the nearby asylum inmates rioted and broke through their restraints and the outer doors.

Deranged, they walked the streets, indistinguishable from the others, dressed as goblins, ghouls, the undead, monsters of every description. Yet no outreached hands could stop them and the havoc, mayhem, chaos, misrule that they fomented. Foaming at the mouth as bipeds, ferocious beasts, ghosts and grave robbers, they thronged at Randolph's steps, admiring handiwork diabolically designed.

One remarked all the candles were red and threw gules of light through vegetable skins. Another ran screaming when in the image at the window she saw what she had become. They were transforming into what they envisaged of themselves without external references. They morphed into pandemonium unwittingly.

Noxious, noisome flesh fell from bones. Rats scurried about in terror. There were also the male figure with the red scythe, the woman in the red mask, the eyeless ones with hands stretched out and waving. This Randolph and his pumpkin witnessed. Then the pumpkins went raving, and the foggy streets boiled and seethed. Bats filled the air, and huge all-devouring insects buzzed.

One muttered that the soul of Cthulhu was approaching and the world would end. Another that he saw the Lord of the Flies and his unholy stinging train. Crows flocked and filled the bare tree branches. Some spread their wings and dropped to an earth so littered with body parts there was no place to land that was not already piled with bones, offal, blood and bile. The stench was maddening.

Carts overloaded with the dead were drawn by the dying. Pyres of stacked corpses awaited matches, but the matchbooks were soggy. The only fire came from Randolph's red candles, fire that jumped to ignite the boy's house as a beacon.

The boy raised his plump hands and showed the stumps where his teeth had been before he hammered them. His face and his pumpkin were coeval twins, looking pained yet smiling with a rectal rictus.

The croaking of frogs began and soon overcame the insect sounds. A running child screamed about the Apocalypse, but only Randolph listened.

He nodded thinking of his sister as the sacrifice. Flagellants flogged each other and themselves in the street that ran by his flaming house. Their trick was to escort Susie to the altar at the street's end where ladders led to a high scaffold. There soulless hangmen draped rotting ropes and guillotines chopped off heads

81

continuously.

Randolph and Susie's parents honked the horn of their car and pressed through the multitudes. They held their ears and shouted, "Where is Susie?" Randolph merely smiled and shrugged. They hurried from the vehicle to their smoldering house, shouting her name repeatedly.

Witches were flying and cackling now, so plenteous that their numbers blocked the moon. Sirens howled and flashing lights competed with red candles. Emergency vehicles circled as the emergencies were widespread. Mothers wept and impotent fathers cursed. The trick-or-treaters demanded treats. They had partaken enough tricks for the night.

Then the factory whistle blew at midnight. The crowd hustled to the prescribed destinations. Fires were extinguished by unseen hands. A deadly silence pervaded the land.

Randolph heard his parents fussing over his sister. She was bawling her brother had caused the wrongs. He stood and walked to the end of the street. He pushed through the overgrown iron gate, which screamed on its unoiled hinges. The bronze mourners seemed to be chanting perpetual masses, to no avail. He entered the family crypt where his own slab received him. And as he lay down to continue his eternal rest, he felt the worm snakes curl around his corpse and lick and eat as they had done before Halloween.

TREASURE HUNTER

A recurring nightmare from my earliest recollections is finding myself pointed down some narrowing shaft to a dead end from which I could not push my body backward, no matter how hard I tried. My father had described his own childhood experience of forcing himself down an animal hole, only to find he could not extricate himself. He survived that ordeal and passed the story to me without emphasis. Now all the horrors come back to me as I hear the rattle of a curled diamondback only inches from my face in the cool, dark tunnel. My boots may be visible to anyone on the trail below if only he or she should look upward. But the place I had found was not obvious. The bonanza was here, to be sure, but I had seconds to enjoy the significance of what I alone had found. I took grim satisfaction that hundreds of thousands of people had dreamed of finding the Lost Dutchman Mine, but only I had broken the code. Now I would take the secret to an unlikely grave.

Bret Halliwell was a treasure hunter. Like most who followed that lonely line of work, he avoided idle company and hiked alone into the wilderness. On a quest, he was an indefatigable researcher, but when he thought he had a bead on a target, he dropped all conversations with outsiders and went for the goal. He was not often mistaken.

Halliwell had the distinction of three significant discoveries to his credit. Most adventurers would have been satisfied with any one of those. The first successful experience—the one that set the hook which held him tantalized to the company of gifted hunters—was the coded pirate treasure, signified by a polyglot, cryptic text on a rock washed by the North Sea. Even learned scholars could not break the code on that godforsaken rock, and many had perished trying to guess what was meant by the directions. Bret had taken one look at the text and shifted his attention to the rock into which it had been chiseled. It was, he thought, a pointer to the goal.

He began digging along the drying line to which the crude obelisk pointed like a crooked finger of fate. Four feet deep he had hit a solid chest. The gold doubloons and precious jewels in the chest comprised a fortune that forever freed the man from want or care. He husbanded the pirate pelf to fund other enterprises which might be even more remunerative. That brought him first to an adventure in the jungles of Belize.

The second discovery for Bret Halliwell was not, as he had initially thought, on the offshore islands that sheltered the Belize coast, but deep inland under ten feet of jungle and soil where an ancient, long-forgotten civilization had been regained by primal vegetation. In the excavations which followed, an entire civilization was visible in outline. The precious remains of inlaid skulls were snapped up by collectors and museums around the world. Again, Halliwell had been above the norm. He had found what no one even thought to look for. And his discovery stimulated a host of ancillary efforts by others. By the time his find became general knowledge, he had moved on, searching this time for treasure buried in English farmland.

Students of the Roman occupation of Britain knew the Roman overlords were wealthy beyond the imaginations of the primitive Britons. Therefore, when the Roman Empire crumbled, spacious estates were left without means of sustenance despite the fact that their managers had large stores of precious metals and jewels.

Heartened by the discoveries of other scavengers— silver and bronze coins, for example—Halliwell systematically identified the largest landowners of late Roman times. The three most promising became his

84

targets, and he funded men and women to use metal detectors over large areas. One of his charges hit pay dirt in a fallow field that had, for generations, seemed to be worthless as farmland. A trove of gold coins from the second and third century AD was split between the British Crown and Bret, with a huge tip for the finder.

After his three magnificent explorations most of his friends, relatives and colleagues thought he would retire to enjoy his fortune, but they did not figure on the dynamics and impact of success in hunting fortunes.

The fourth venture, finding the Lost Dutchman Mine, seemed to Halliwell the pinnacle of a career punctuated by privation and spiced with determination. He thought he could beat the opposition; he held forth at meetings of fellow treasure hunters, deriding the attempts of others and boasting that only he had what it took to find the fabled mine.

At a meeting of five hundred treasure hunters, who paid the handsome sum of five thousand dollars each to hear his wisdom, the guru of treasure hunters described what they were all looking for.

He said, "Imagine roseate quartz so beaded by lightning-melted gold that the aureate drops resemble copious tears. Then think that the veins of quartz and gold dive so deep underground that one man with intelligence and gumption could mine that vein his entire life and not exhaust the discovery."

The audience was enraptured by Halliwell], and they sprang to their feet when he had finished giving his speech. Though they crowded the dais to garner additional information which would set themselves apart from the others, the guru had nothing further to say. His audience felt he had given them plenty of

85

advice to pursue their goals. But one intrepid fortune hunter refused to be satisfied. Her name was Rapunzel Smith.

That night at the Hilton where the event had been held, Rapunzel knocked on Brett's door and ingratiated herself upon the master. By the next morning, she felt she had earned the right to be the man's equal partner. As a consequence, she became his shadow, following him wherever he went. He laughed when anyone remarked on her being a gold digger, for her reputation preceded her. Rapunzel had married three miners and had driven them all to heart attacks, trying to satisfy her unusual lust—for gold and other things of extreme value, such as kimberlite diamond lodes and emerald mines.

Nevertheless, Brett Halliwell had an abiding fervor to find the Lost Dutchman Mine, but now he had to contend with a strong-willed, sexy woman urging him on like a Classical Fury. She would not let him rest. When he came out of the desert after one of his expeditions, she rode him hard until he was on the road again to investigate another site. True, he was visibly florid from his physical exertions, but he was driven now like a man possessed. Some said Rapunzel's insatiable lust was affecting his judgment. The other treasure hunters began to see the man in a new light. If Rapunzel had made him a target for her attentions, they thought they should also pay particular regard to the man and his movements.

It soon transpired that Halliwell could not set out on an expedition without twenty or so disciples following in his wake. He had to strategize to lose his fellow travelers before he homed in on his objective. He was gratified that the same fate had beset the 'Dutchman' for whom the objective had derived its name. His problem was articulated by his lascivious partner.

"Face it, Bret,' she said. 'You are either the most brilliant deception artist who ever set his sights on the Lost Dutchman Mine, or you are the biggest fraud in the fortune hunting game. I'm getting tired providing you comfort time when you are not prospecting. Either get to your business, or I'm going to hitch my wagon to another rising star."

Halliwell, who was already doing his level best to find the bonanza, despaired of finding his quest. He withdrew for a few weeks and studied all the available evidence with fresh eyes. Accounts of other fortune hunters were plentiful, but none of those had achieved their goal. Repeatedly, he read how would-be discoverers had gravitated either to the Vulture Mine or to Superstition Mountain. Theories about the Vulture Mine were reduced to piracy:

The Dutchman had stolen the riches of the most productive mine in the history of Arizona to provide the samples he brought back from his secret mine to fund his livelihood. The theories about Superstition Mountain were reduced to the common trajectory the Dutchman took every time he returned to Phoenix with bonanza gold, ore so rich that it paralleled none found anywhere else.

One night, in the middle of tumultuous lovemaking, Halliwell had his Eureka moment! He leapt up from the bed he had been sharing with Rapunzel and ran to the shower. She was angry to have her orgasms interrupted but excited that her man had finally made a discovery which might turn out to be meaningful. She stood outside the shower stall with a towel in her hand.

"I surely hope your discovery is worth your having left my arms to shower."

Halliwell smiled enigmatically and accepted the towel. He dried himself hurriedly and dressed without saying anything. He threw together provisions and went out back to saddle his mule. As he walked out of the yard with his mule on a tether behind him, he heard Rapunzel's shrieking.

"You bastard! If you don't return with the gold this time, you can forget having another night of love with me. I hope you find the Dutchman's prize or die in the attempt."

The only response the termagant got was a shake of her lover's head and a hand gesture that must have meant, "Aroint thee, witch!" or some such. Rapunzel resolved to pack her things and leave.

Meanwhile, Bret Halliwell felt rather than saw his followers picking up his trail. Instead of heading directly for his goal, he traced Hopi patterns until the disciples left off and gave up. Some hoped to intercept the hunter's trail when he returned from his expedition. Others went back to his dwelling where they encamped, waiting for his return there. Like the gold-digger Rapunzel, their patience was at an end. More than one of Halliwell's competitors thought evilly about killing the man and stealing his hoard.

Halliwell did not take the public entrance into Superstition Mountain Park. As it happened, the black clouds and twisters provided good cover, which sheets of rain improved. Thus, the treasure hunter entered the labyrinthine paths of Superstition with forked lightning jagging down from the sky. He knew where he was going to begin taking samples. When he reached the place, he observed the way the pouring rain cascaded off the primeval rock and knew he had finally placed a winning bet.

To demonstrate that his hunch was correct, he sampled the pieces of rock on either side of the temporary waterfall which nature had provided. He was glad to see his samples showed the greatest bounty directly under the fall. That could only signify the mother lode lay above him along the line of the waterfall. He did not wait for the rain to stop. He tethered his mule to a rock and began scaling the precipice with nothing more than his hand pick and a leather sampling bag. By the time he was thirty feet above the trail where the mule stood stalwart, the rain had stopped. The rocks still dripped, but he could now see by sunlight where he was heading.

Halliwell continued climbing. He was so excited about his discovery, he had to take deep breaths to calm down. He didn't realize he was being watched until a rifle shot struck so near his face that the rock shrapnel struck him in the neck and shoulder. He did not stop climbing. In fact, he was now convinced he had to divert his shooter's perspective and focus him on a false premise.

"Damn it all,' he called out to the hidden person. 'You missed me. If you kill me, you'll never find the mine you're looking for."

"Halliwell,' the concealed shooter yelled back, 'you know you led me to the gold. If I dropped you now, I'd find the mine in days or weeks. Admit you've been bested."

"You are much deceived. I'm only playing a hunch. But it's one of a half dozen that play the same way. Only one of my hunches can provide the pay dirt. So shoot me. I don't care. I've made three fortunes. This would only be my fourth."

The rifleman fired again, only the shot went wide of his intended target.

Halliwell heard the voice of Rapunzel saying, "I know you are onto something, Bret. Do you hear me?" Her voice echoed off the canyon walls, so he could not estimate her position.

"I hear you. And I say again that I have a vague sense of what will work. Five other sites must be investigated to find the truth."

"When you're done here, we'll be down here on the ground below where you now are waiting to accompany you to your next priority and so forth until you've tried everything." Rapunzel was almost mocking him.

"When you say 'we,' what folks besides you are waiting down there?"

"You may not know Ike, Sam and Luke. We have had great hopes for you. Surely, your strike will be large enough to satisfy all four of us as well as yourself."

Halliwell guessed the score immediately which was he had been betrayed by the woman. He climbed past a small opening in the cliff. He used the opening as a toehold, but he did not hesitate there. He climbed another twenty feet before he tapped at the rock with his pick to take a sample and put it in his leather pouch. He slowly made his way down the precipice, careful not to pay attention to the opening to the mine so the secret remained his own. When he reached the ground, he loosened the tether and walked his mule back down the path and out of the labyrinth. He thought about what he was doing,

I am a dead man as soon as I give an indication that I have found the Lost Dutchman Mine. I'll lead Rapunzel and her three partners away and try to lose them as I visit five other sites. I don't expect they'll want to second guess me. Their kind is too greedy to want to do work for their gain.

Halliwell noticed that the four thieves rode in his wake as he led them on a merry chase to the north of Phoenix to the Vulture Mine. He puttered about in the slag heaps outside that fruitful mine and left his pouch on the top of one heap while he slowly led his mule into a blind canyon where he climbed to the top on a winding ledge that the animal could navigate. He saw how Rapunzel and the three men stopped to pick up the leather case and examine its contents. Even at this distance, he could hear his erstwhile lover's voice.

"Hey Ike and Luke, will you take a look at what I've found. Look at these beads of gold in this roseate quartz."

Halliwell smiled as he raised his rifle and fired three shots at the bell that stood outside the main entrance of the Vulture Mine, That bell was rung when thieves were apprehended stealing the mine's ore. Three heavily-armed men appeared out of nowhere to get the drop on the four would-be outlaws. To be caught red-handed incurred heavy penalties, so Rapunzel dropped the bag and distanced herself from it. She did not act fast enough to avoid detection. One of the Vulture security men picked up the pouch and held it in the air.

"Keep these four desperadoes covered, men. This pouch full of ore will consign these four thieves to long prison terms. In an earlier time, we would have strung them up from the hanging tree over there."

"Clem, what's prohibiting us from doing that right now?" asked one of his aides.

"I'm not fool enough to do that when we don't know who struck the bell that informed on these varmints."

All seven figures looked around but could not see Halliwell or his mule. That was because the treasure hunter had begun to depart the vicinity. He moved slowly to avoid detection. When he thought he had put sufficient distance between himself and the Vulture Mine, he threaded himself through the landscape, edging back toward Superstition Mountain and the real source of the ore.

He decided to take his time returning to the precipice where he knew the gold could be found. He thought Rapunzel and her henchmen would be inconvenienced but not stinted by his ploy. He therefore had to count on the thieves posting bail and getting back on his trail.

Halliwell walked his mule for a week, with random changes of direction. He enjoyed living in the open and sleeping under the stars at night. He liked the rain in the monsoon season especially because it was a natural shower. This time when he entered Superstition Mountain, it was night and no inclement weather threatened. It was a time for the migration of scorpions.

The first indications he had of the arthropods were the absence of cricket sounds and the crunch of insects under his boots. The path seemed to be blanketed with the stinging creatures, but he had long experience with them when they sought new homes by migrating. As he hoisted himself up the precipice that led to the bonanza, Bret knew they would not follow him. However, he still watched for scorpions on each ledge and foothold. By the time he reached the hole where the gold was to be found, he knew his only lethal problems would be gila monsters and snakes. In fact, just inside the opening was a gila, which he dislodged with his knife and pushed out the opening and down the cliff. He slid into the declivity where the next observable object, just inside the opening on the floor, was a skeleton in Indian clothing. The bones shattered when he touched them.

Halliwell realized that the Indian remains were confirmation of his hunch that he had found the Lost Dutchman Mine. He removed his boots and left them at the opening as they would do him no good service where he was heading. As he continued to crawl down the narrow path, he recalled being tutored by a man who claimed to have been the descendant of an Indian and a Conquistador. At the time of their meeting, they talked about gold. The old man had told him that no Indian would trade in gold since it was unlucky—and a sacrilege. Of course, he had said, 'All us Indians know where the gold is hidden.' He had then laughed at the idea that any white man could endure what was required to find it, much less mine it.

Halliwell's pen light failed, and he was now crawling in the dark. He took out his cigarette lighter and flicked it. The light showed where the quartz lay in a wide swath on the narrow path. Smiling, he continued following the gold.

He had slithered another fifty yards when he heard shouting from outside the opening. The shrieking voice was Rapunzel's. The chorus in back of her words were her three male companions.

"I know you're in there, Bret. Are you going to crawl back out, or do I have to come in there after you?"

Halliwell called back, "I'm busy. Why don't you find something interesting to do with your three toyboys by the entrance while I do my job."

"You bastard. You gave us up to those toughs at the Vulture Mine. That was not kosher of you. I'm afraid you have now lost your right to your fair share of this gold. Besides, you lied. This was the first place you came, and the gold was here after all. I should have finished you when I had you in my rifle sight."

"When I saw the scorpions marching up the path, I knew you would be near at hand."

"Ha ha. Very funny. Well, Bret, your humor is lost on my friends."

Three shots were fired, and Rapunzel's voice stopped.

Halliwell said, "Rapunzel, are you still there?"

"She will not be with you for the rest of your life, Bret Halliwell. She was right about one thing—you won't be rewarded with a share. Lead will be your recompense. Your lady fair is lying on top of an Indian's skeleton. She'll doubtless find solace in him that she never found in you—or in Ike or Luke here for that matter." The three men laughed raucously.

"It must be Sam talking. Am I right?"

"You guessed right, Bret. Are you going to back out of there, or am I going to have to crawl in and drag you out?"

Halliwell heard the three men whispering, but he could not make out what they were saying.

"Gentlemen, I cannot make out anything you are saying. I can tell you one thing: I am definitely not going to crawl back out. I guess you're going to have to come after me." He scuttled forward, feeling his way as the opening narrowed.

"Well, it looks like only Ike and I will be sharing the wealth. And I am coming after you just in case you know about a secret back way through the mountain." Sam was sounding smug.

"What's the matter? Did Luke get cold feet?"

"That's one way of putting the situation. Luke died with an arrow in his back. Damned Indians. Who knew? Say, Halliwell, are the Indians with you?"

"My advice to you is to retrace your steps and climb back down the precipice before the Indians kill you all."

Ike hollered, "Aimee. I'm hit."

Sam's voice indicated fear as he shouted, "What is going on here? Ike, are you just wounded, or what?"

Ike wailed, "I have an arrow in my back. The shaft is scraping the top of the entrance, and it makes my back hurt like hell."

"Well, Ike, if you're going to die, do so quietly. And I remind you that you'll get no share if you die."

"I'm not laughing with you, Sam."

Bret heard three shots fired in quick succession.

"Bastard. You've killed me. And now you'll have to deal with Halliwell with that arrow in your back."

"Shut up and die, Sam." He fired a fourth shot, and

Bret heard nothing more from Sam.

"Well, Ike, it's just you and me. And now you'll need me to help you get down the cliff to a doctor."

"I'm not going to need help from you." He fired two shots and Bret heard him reloading and breathing heavily.

"You can't kill all the Indians, Ike. You don't know how many of them are out there."

"I can hold out till daylight. Then someone in authority will find me."

"I wouldn't count on that, Ike."

"What would you do in my place?"

"Pray. Or you could put down your gun and let me bargain with the Indians."

"That's rich. So how would you bargain?"

"First, I'd say I would not touch the gold we have found because it's unlucky."

"Fat chance of that, Halliwell. I've worked hard to find this gold, and people have died in the process. I'm not going to die for nothing."

"In my limited experience, I think that's exactly what most people die for, and you'll be no exception to the rule."

"I refuse to die."

"Then relinquish the thought of owning the gold."

"Never."

"Then you'll get your just reward."

Ike was silent.

"Ike, are you still with the living?"

The opening was silent. Bret flicked on his lighter and descended deeper into the path. He saw how the gold shimmered in the light. It was now not beaded in quartz. The gold was like a frozen river in the rock. The river was widening now. Halliwell had never seen a seam of gold so wide. Just when he realized the scope of his discovery, his lighter failed which was when he first heard the rattle.

"Ike, if you're conscious, you might enjoy the irony of my situation. I am inches from a diamondback rattlesnake. It is coiled and ready to strike. Do you hear me, Ike?"

Now Halliwell heard nothing but the rattle. If Ike was still alive, he was incapable of speaking.

Bret Halliwell chuckled when he struggled to push his body backward up the path——and failed. Before the snake struck, a phrase he had learned in junior high school Latin kept ringing in his ears: *Radix malorum est cupiditas.*

THE ET EEL INFESTATION

As an NYPD homicide officer dedicated to fighting alien attackers, Val Cassidy was accustomed to viewing scenes of grisly murder victims. Even so, the bloody scene in Central Park was enough to turn the veteran's stomach. The vic was a fully-clothed Caucasian brunette female between twenty-five and forty-two years of age. She was wearing a colorful jogging outfit, including expensive trainers. The distinctive feature of her body was the absence of anything from her pelvic and abdominal cavities, which were empty.

The homicide department had called Cassidy after two independent witnesses claimed to have seen the woman voluntarily wade into the water before she made motions and noises of a young woman in the terminal phase of pregnancy. She held her stomach and screamed until she passed out and lay still. The witnesses noticed a pool of blood in the water around her, which seemed to be boiling like a frothy red stew. When Cassidy arrived at the scene, the water was its normal color. The only distinction was the large number of tiny fish milling in the general area of the body.

A police photographer was busy taking pictures as the detective waded into the pool to get a first impression close up. He used surgical gloves and his pen to lift the vic's soggy sweatshirt and pants. Right away he observed the bottom of the women's pants had been neatly cut away. Once the photographer had finished his on-site photos, Cassidy waved to the ambulance crew to move in and extract the corpse for transfer to the morgue. Dripping from the waist down, he supervised the extraction until the ambulance doors closed and the vehicle drove off to the morgue with no lights flashing.

Val arrived at his warehouse office and went straight to the shower enclosure with not a word to Mabel Deuce, who saw by the way his eyes rolled and his head shivered he had seen something he wished he could unsee. He finished his shower, put his wet work clothes in the washer and dressed in the spare set he kept in a locker. He then picked up six darts from his desk and hurled them at a target he had made after the Scionite Affair. "I wish these darts could find the vital parts of the perp who killed that young lady whose body we found in Central Park this morning."

"This is the first I've heard of this murder. Want to talk about it?"

"Yes, but I have to contact Dr. Sundt on the secure line before I start conjecturing. Please get her on the secure line for me ASAP."

Mabel got lucky as Sundt answered on the first ring. She passed the phone to her boss and showed him the indicator that the line could handle TOP SECRET– CAVEAT traffic.

"Dr. Sundt speaking."

"You know from your phone's Caller ID this is Val Cassidy and the line is set to TS-Caveat. I need your assistance assigning a caveat and participating in an autopsy at the New York city morgue."

"What are the facts?"

For five minutes Cassidy put the federal agent in the picture. She remained silent for another three minutes before she said, 'Eeler' is the caveat. I have placed three cases in that caveat during the last two weeks."

"Can you tell me more?"

"All the vics had lost their intestines. Two had burst so a flood of eels in a bloody mass emerged from their bodies in their final phase of transformation. The third died in the Nile River in Egypt after a lanky green monster stepped out of her abdomen and sank below the surface with the corpse."

"Do you have any leads on the perp besides the eels?"

"The only lead we have is the eels, but they do not appear to be *ordinary* eels. And the vic in the Nile seems to have been some sort of priestess of an ancient eel-worshipping cult tracing its roots to Egypt before the dynastic periods began. From what the experts tell me, the cult is linked to chthonic deities like snakes which must be propitiated with bowls of milk or oil."

"If the cult is that old, why haven't we heard about more victims through the ages?"

"Again, the experts tell me the astrological signs have only just aligned as they did ten thousand years ago."

"So, some obscure prophecy is being fulfilled, and we won't know what's really happening till we have a Khufu boat full of bodies without entrails on our case list."

"Two other details will amuse you while I catch the first plane to New York. The first is the miraculous escape of a lanky green creature from one of our most secret labs. The second is the odd case of a splinter group of the eel cult at what used to be the College of William and Mary in Virginia."

"I have a headache trying to collate all the facts. Maybe you can enlighten me once you have reached the morgue. I will delay the opening of the body till you arrive. You might like to eat before you climb on your plane. You might not want to do much eating after you see the corpse."

"Val, you know I live for this kind of weird event. Please say hello to Mabel for me."

In the background Mabel said, "Thank you, Dr. Sundt. I'll look forward to seeing you again later today."

-"While Sundt is in transit, go down to the New York

99

Public Library and find what you can about chthonic deities, the eel cult, eviscerations by murderers and any links of these subjects to the College of William and Mary."

"I'm on my way, boss. Do you want me to meet you at the morgue?"

"Absolutely not. Come back here when the library closes."

"I'm history."

"Not yet! I know how much you like doing obscure research. Don't get lost in it. And if you have a strange impulse to seek a pond to unload, just call me on my cell before you do."

"Very funny!"

Cassidy pulled the darts out of his target, whereupon he moved back by his desk and hurled the darts into the target again. He assessed his marksmanship and then "rinsed and repeated," as Mabel was accustomed to saying. An hour before the scheduled opening at the morgue, he received a call from the forensic pathologist requesting his instructions.

"We are going to wait for the arrival of Dr. Sundt before we begin the dissection. Have the chemists done their analyses? I hope to present the illustrious doctor from Washington with the results this afternoon. I will be arriving there within the hour."

"You might want to know that the corpse's condition is the mirror image of two others I have dissected in the last month. Both of those were Jane Does assigned to homicide and forgotten."

"Please gather whatever reports and notes you have on those priors for Dr. Sund's perusal."

Cassidy was fuming, but there was nothing he could do about the failures of personnel in the NYPD. Unidentified persons inevitably had a shelf life of ten days. Then the cases became cold and the remains were cremated.

As he drove to the morgue, Val pounded on his steering wheel each time he thought about the possibility a serial killer on the model of the Black Dahlia was stalking the streets of his city. He wondered how many other vics would pop onto his personal radar screen once he and Mabel really began digging for instances with similarities to the current one.

Dr. Sundt had not arrived at he morgue, but the pathologist had brought the records of the other two cases. Cassidy noted both corpses had been found naked, clogging sewer filters in the center of the city. As the young man had described, the decaying bodies had evidence of massive evacuation of the pelvic area. The photographs showed a level of decomposition that would make identification almost impossible without the assistance of special techniques and vast databases like those at Dr. Sundt's command.

Cassidy and Dr. Christopher, the pathologist, played gin rummy while they waited for their version of the Iceman. When she did enter the room, Sundt took charge and announced she and her people were going to take the corpse to her private, secret lab in Washington. When she learned two additional corpses of the same description were still in the morgue, she appropriated the paperwork and set her people to removing the Jane Does' remains. As her men labored, she moved to the operating room and observed as Dr. Christopher performed his autopsy. As he cut into the various areas of the corpse, he outlined what the chemical analysis had revealed.

"As in the other two cases, the disembowelment here corresponds to the area containing the intestines and reproductive organs. Lacerations indicate the attack on the pelvic floor was made from the inside so, when the breakthrough occurred, the pulpy mass emerged in the

101

same fashion as a birth. Remarkable is the thoroughness of the evacuation. Of course, all three vics died in water. Drowning was not a cause of death."

Dr. Sundt agreed.

When Christopher had completed his operation, the secret men removed the parts of the body in a body bag, as they had for the other two bodies. Dr. Sundt nodded, and they were gone.

"Dr. Christopher, thank you. Please make copies of your report for my files." She handed him her business card. "If you should come across any further vics with the same signature, please call me right away. Now, Mr. Cassidy, let's segue to your place. We will have to stop on the way for one of your New York hot dogs with sauerkraut and mustard. You cannot believe how hungry I get watching an autopsy."

Val drove Dr. Sundt to his office where Mabel had already returned from her research mission to the NY Public Library. She had made voluminous copies taken from books and manuscripts owned by the library. While Dr. Sundt ate her hot dog, Mabel reported what she had found to her boss and her guest. When she finished, Sundt asked Val and her to sign the briefing papers for the caveat. They signed the documents and Sundt briefed them on the substance, neatly including what she had learned at the autopsy.

Cassidy was most interested in her story about the green figure as he knew how to kill that kind of monster with his darts. "I take it you captured the creature to do experiments on it?"

"That was our intent, yes. We were impressed by its uncanny intelligence. We must have underestimated what it was capable of. All the time it was in our custody, it was scoping out its escape. We should have suspected it would have help on the outside and that it could communicate with its rescuers."

"How specific can you be about the rescue?"

"The creature was kept in an aquarium except for one hour a day when it was allowed to roam freely about the campus. Adjacent to the grounds was a dam, whose causeway ran to a holding tank. The creature decided to climb the electric fence at a time it had been deactivated for maintenance. It jumped from the barbed wire at the top of the fence thirty feet straight down so it landed in the causeway. It rolled to the exhaust drain and slithered to the holding pond at the bottom where it swam to the opposite side. There an unmarked van was waiting to pick it up."

"It was certainly not an eel. How does it come into the picture of thousands of small eels lurking inside human bowels for their form of breakout?"

"I am going to have to conjecture to give you an answer to your question. I believe the green monster is an extraterrestrial being, infiltrated into earth for the purpose of preparing the planet as a platform for invasion. The eels are not terrestrial eels but ET conduits that are somehow ingested live into humans where they mature till they are ready for the next stage of their mission."

"So they used an ancient cult and its rituals to multiply and survive till they were numerous enough to take over whatever was necessary to make invasion a cake walk."

"That's right, Mabel. If I had one, I would give you a cigar as a reward for your correct deduction!"

"So tell us, Dr. Sundt, how do we kill these murderous, invading bastards?"

Sundt pursed her lips and said, "I think the key is the green monster. Think of it as a she, capable of reproducing eels infinitely, yet requiring sequestration, occasionally, in the receptive entrails of a human."

Cassidy began throwing his darts at the Scionite target again. His mind was reeling from the inputs he had received. He had to breathe deeply to manage his anger. "There may be billions of little eels in our water and sewer systems now. What do you propose we do?"

"Washington is planning a campaign to discourage the ingestion of live eels. As for the green monster, we are working on a project that will detect this creature wherever it lives. The sensors will be positioned so as not to interfere with normal human activity, and they will not have a strong enough impulse to harm a fetus."

Mabel was puzzled. "If the eels in question are already in our reservoirs and sewage systems, how can they be removed?"

Val nodded and looked to Dr. Sundt for the answer.

"We believe the ET eels must be implanted in a human two to three weeks after evacuation from a human, or they perish. This adaptation was designed to allow humans a minimal time to capture and analyze the invaders and to keep their collective focus on reaching a safe harbor."

Val said, "We can therefore assume the eel cult is still an important part of their life cycle. The cult members are the agents who convey the eels to the digestive tracts of humans, and they prepare the carriers of the green monsters for reception of them."

"Only among fanatics will the desire to preserve the progenitors of the ET eels be stronger than the will to survive. We have, therefore, attempted to locate all eel cult enclaves, and we have narrowed those down to the one hundred die-hard groups. Our agents are infiltrating each group separately, but the going is slow. I have a printout in my office showing the leaders of the extremist cult membership. These women and men are the likeliest to be offered the privilege of bearing the future of the ET race."

"I presume, Dr. Sundt, the majority of the die-hards live right here in New York?

"In fact, they are distributed evenly between New York and Cairo with outliers in places as distant as Borneo and Mali. The outliers are being dealt with separately. I am focusing my efforts on Egypt as the initial location of the ancient cult. I am hoping you will cover New York. The American Southwest is the next most probable location."

"May I volunteer to cover that area?" Mabel asked.

Dr. Sundt smiled. "It is good of you to volunteer, Mabel, but Dr. Christopher has already signed up for that part. He is married to a Hopi Indian who can help us gain access wherever required. I am sure Mr. Cassidy requires your services checking out the New York contingent of the eel cult. Am I right, Val?"

"Absolutely. Besides, I think everyone involved should travel in pairs, given the dangers of not doing so. Dr. Sundt, you also mentioned a cult organization at the College of William and Mary."

"Thank you for reminding me. A professor of anthropology there is also a devotee of the eel cult claiming to be the first such in America. He was visited by an old student who claimed to be in Williamsburg to visit classmates. After three days, she was on her way to the train station when she waved the professor down from her cab and asked him to help her pay what she owed to the cabbie and the hotel. He immediately turned to use his credit card to make the payments, but when he swung back the woman had disappeared. Not only that, she had taken off her clothes and wandered to the nearest stream. The professor reported her as a missing person to the police, but the woman in question was listed as deceased four years prior. Further, when the police visited the professor's listed residence to ask further questions, he had gone missing too."

"What about the young woman's classmates?"

"After interviewing all of those who had seen her during her visit, the police drew up a schedule of her activities before she left Williamsburg. She had attended a meeting of the eel cult at which a ceremonial event was eating raw eels. Naturally, we have the five young woman who ate the eels under close medical observation. An APB has been issued for the professor. I am afraid that is the limit of our authority."

"Do you have any further leads for us to follow—any at all?"

"I have a long shot. A young designer on Long Island does some pretty weird covers for underground literature houses. Among the most recent of those is a cover that fairly depicts the culmination of a cult meeting where a woman in Egyptian costume is opening her mouth for an eel as she rubs her stomach and closes her eyes in delight. Here is the address of the woman in question. She often lives with an unemployed companion and a cat." She handed Val a slip of paper with an address of a trailer park on the island.

Dr. Sundt bade Val and Mabel goodbye and hurried back to Washington.

The next morning the intrepid homicide detective and his assistant drove up to the tip of the island to visit the address of the graphic artist.

The trailer park did not look like the venue of an exclusive club devoted to eel worship. Junk littered the entire park, and detritus from the last a hurricane remained where it had lain after the storm had passed three months ago.

A knock on the trailer door brought a burst of

invective followed by, "Go away, damn you. I don't have any money to buy anything. In fact, I don't have any money to pay my bills."

When Val knocked again and said, "Police homicide. Open the door or I will kick it in."

The young woman's tone changed instantly. "Just a minute, Officer! I am trying to corral my cat. There. Turn the handle and pull the door open."

"I am sorry to disturb you unannounced, Ma'am, but my partner and I would like to ask you a few questions about a murder."

"Murder? What murder?"

"The murder that was discovered in Central Park yesterday morning," Mabel replied.

The young woman laughed and asked the police to come in and sit on the couch. "Would you like some Nescafé?

Half empty coffee cups littered the coffee table, and the sink was full of stacked dishes that looked at least two weeks old.

"Specifically, we want to ask about a cover image you did for *Weird and Weirder Magazine*. Mabel observed the woman's face screw up as if she were struggling to remember the cover. The silence in the trailer was palpable. The cat meowed from its carrier. The girl's boyfriend entered from a bedroom, dressed only in his underwear.

"Robert, these people are from the police. They have questions for us."

"I haven't done anything criminal, lately."

"Shut up. This is apparently about a murder in Central Park. And they have been asking about my latest cover image."

Val and Mabel sat like as immobile as statues and listened.

"Why don't you just tell them who you did the cover

for."

"I Photoshopped the image from a picture of the gathering of a cult about eels."

"Do you have the original picture from which you made the Photoshopped image?" Mable asked.

The young woman stopped what she was doing in the kitchen and picked up the picture from her desk and handed it to Mabel.

"The central figure is Mother Night. She is the leader of the group. The names of her group members are on the reverse of the photo. Do you think she might have been involved in the murder?"

"We have no idea. We are in the early stages of our investigation. Are you a member of the eel cult?" asked Val.

The young woman and her boyfriend erupted in laughter. She said, "Certainly not. We may be messy, but we aren't daft."

"What do you mean by that?"

"Well, first, we don't think the world is going to end anytime soon like the eelers do. Second, we have precious little money, which is what it takes to belong to a group like that. Mother Night lives above Central Park in an apartment complex for the super rich. Pardon me, but no one in this trailer right now could afford to be involved."

Mabel inquired, "So how did you get the privilege of providing the cover image?"

"I get orders from every kind of person, rich and poor. I am fast and good but not cheap or we would not be able to pay the rent and electricity."

"Do you have Mother Night's address?"

Robert looked sheepish. He put Mother Night's embossed business card on the coffee table in the last of the available space. "Don't ask me how I got that card. Investigations are the only way I can help Heidi do her work. You see, I check out the folks who offer to pay her for her services. Not everyone is credit worthy."

Val smiled. "Let's say I was able to get into Mother Night's apartment without tripping the alarms. What would I find inside?"

Robert dipped his head down and raised his eyes up at the same time. "You'd find a posh apartment with everything anyone who loved eels would covet. For example, in the middle of the living room is an enormous aquarium full of the critters that give off a neon green glow, and in the middle bedroom is another aquarium with the most beautiful green creature swimming back and forth, rhythmically sloshing in the tank. More live eels are in the fridge, but I would not touch the slimy things. Of course, money is everywhere if that's what you want. In the cabinets are stacks of bills of every denomination, all unmarked. On the walls are pictures of eel groups from all over the world. Then there are some advanced tech devices I had never seen.

"I don't suppose you know anyone who could get the two of us policemen into that apartment without setting off the alarms. Would you?"

The young man fidgeted. Seeing the steely look in Cassidy 's eyes, he said, "And if I did, why should I turn that knowledge into a jail sentence.?"

Cassidy smiled ironically. "Let's say I have a Get Out of Jail Free card that comes with the one thousand dollars I would pay for this simple service, no questions asked."

Heidi whistled. "Could you make that two thousand in unmarked bills?"

"What about admissibility, Mr. Policeman? Once you gained admittance, you could not use anything you found inside in a court of law."

109

"To answer your question, Heidi, two thousand for an in-and-out visit is okay by me. And Robert, who said any of this is going to court, ever?

Robert said, "I think we are close to a deal. I'd like to see the cash first, naturally, and I'd need to know the times of entry and exit."

The four conspirators discussed the nitty-gritty details of the B&E adventure they planned. Val happened to have two thousand in unmarked bills in his suit coat pocket. He handed Heidi half of the cash as earnest money, the rest being due after the successful exit.

As Val and Mabel rose to leave, Heidi's eyes teared up. "Mister and Ma'am, I don't know who you are or where you are going with our help, but I feel we're doing the first really decent thing we have done in ten years. It is good. I know it in my heart. And if we can ever help again, please do not hesitate to ask."

As they drove back to their office through the late afternoon sunlight, Val waxed poetically. "Though they are doing us a favor for money, those two are good kids who deserve a chance."

"Let's get through this operation in one piece, boss. Then maybe you can propose marriage to me, and I will show you how to celebrate."

Val and Mabel had agreed on many occasions to keep marriage off the table, so their silence was palpable all the way south. When they got back to the office, Mabel drafted a plan of action. Val went back to throwing his darts at his target.

As the plan unfolded, the list of players grew to include Dr. Sundt and her team, the New York Fire Department and four ambulances, two of which were fitted out with aquaria.

The entry into the apartment of Mother Night went flawlessly. The layout and contents of the apartment were exactly as Robert had described them. Val and

Mabel hid in the linen closet after Val called in a fire alarm. Mother Night and her companion of the evening, a professor of anthropology at the College of William and Mary, were arrested—him for being a fugitive of the law and her for harboring a fugitive.

More importantly, the two aquaria were carried to the freight elevator and thence conveyed to the two ambulances with similar aquaria built in inside the vehicles. A money laundering unit confiscated the cash in the apartment while Dr. Sundt's crew harvested the photographs that hung on the walls. She also took into custody curious communication devices, the likes of which the US intelligence agencies were going to salivate over for years to come.

When the raid had ended, everything of value to law enforcement and intelligence was held in custody.

Descending in the main elevator to the lobby of the apartment complex, Val found Robert waiting to collect his thousand dollars, which Val paid in a handoff that would have made a brush-pass master applaud.

Back in their office, Val and Mabel popped the cork on a bottle of chilled champagne. Dr. Sundt arrived in time to share a fluted glass of the bubbly before she was off to Washington.

"I don't suppose I should ask how you managed to find Mother Night's apartment on the very night when the William and Mary professor was shacking up with her?"

"No, you shouldn't. But thank you for reminding me. I have one more call to make.

After dialing a number, he heard, "This is Heidi."

"This is Val Cassidy. I just want to thank you for helping. Robert has full payment for what we owe you. You will never know how important your contribution was tonight, but it was everything you suspected. Best

111

of luck to you and your boyfriend." He hung up and returned to Mabel, who was saying goodbye to Dr. Sundt.

"Val, I will be back when we have interrogated Mother Night and assessed all the data from every source. Be ready to travel, as I suspect the eel cult to be decentralized for its command and control and survivable. If I am not wrong, Cairo is our next area of interest. Maybe Mabel should see the Pyramids and take a Nile cruise?"

Naturally, Mabel wanted to check into a hotel, but Val counselled vigilance. "Remember how glad we were after our last triumph over the Scionites. Then the ET alien escaped and came after me here."

"A girl can dream, can't she? Oh well, I'll call in a pizza—large with extra cheese and pepperoni. What do you think?"

He raised two thumbs. Then he went back to throwing darts at his target.

HER PARTIAL PRESENCE

Private investigator Val Cassidy's girlfriend Mabel Deuce went missing during the most recent redistribution event. He was convinced that Mabel was not an extra-terrestrial alien, but who could know for sure? Following the trail of her last few days, the detective discovered an eerie pattern of disappearances among her friends and associates. He also detected rumors of his own disappearance and had the distinct feeling he was being shadowed, perhaps stalked. He sensed the presence of menacing free-range tentacles. The lurking aliens seemed to be communicating, but he could not interpret their expressions. Was Mabel talking *through* the aliens?

One night in a dream his girlfriend appeared in a costume of numerous tentacles. She informed him of her transformation and invited him to surrender to the aliens so they could be together again, forever. Cassidy awakened in a cold sweat. He showered and dressed, determined to penetrate the alien presence.

He carried his dart weapons, which had taken care of the Scionite alien. The tentacles dropped from buildings and surrounded him, but he resisted until he ran out of darts. Overcome, he felt soft hands caressing his face.

He was lying on the pavement alone except for the hands of his girlfriend and her eyes. He could not tell whether the sounds he heard were his or her screams. But he knew he was awake, and as much of Mabel was with him as was possible under the circumstances.

THE MUSIC MASTER OF
NORTH ELEVENTH STREET

The three most notable features of North Eleventh Street in Allentown are the large number of musicians living there, the evanescent presences haunting the street day and night and the number of serious photographers. These separate communities do not commingle generally, but the most perceptible is the musicians.

On a summer's afternoon when the row homes have their windows open on account of the heat, you can hear pianos, trumpets, piccolos, violins, drums and clarinets making their unique sounds while taking no notice of the others. Only the discerning passerby who favored music would grasp the cacophony of the whole as one mad, continuous composition.

At the end of the row across from the cemetery was Dr. Fiedler's dwelling, where young violinists and violists arrived at half-hour intervals weekday afternoons and all day Saturday for lessons. Sunday afternoons the Lehigh Valley String Quartet practiced their repertoire and had high tea.

Fiedler was first chair violinist in the Valley Symphony Orchestra. His melodious instrument was one of the six hundred and fifty surviving genuine Stradivarius violins. As a result, the cognoscenti gathered whenever he played in public. Once each quarter in the evening, he gave a concert at the Athenaeum Conservatory accompanied by Miss Delia Crawford. Proceeds from these performances went to music scholarships for local talent and for musical instruments for the local middle- and high school bands and orchestras.

Fiedler was a serious musician with many composer friends who lived in the Middle Atlantic States and

114

abroad. He made it his mission to conduct groups of young people whenever invited to do so. Among his contacts with musicians throughout the Lehigh Valley numbered the best and brightest rising stars. A recommendation from Fiedler stood a candidate a good chance of acceptance at the Julliard School in New York where only 7% of applicants were admitted.

I knew Dr. Fiedler because he had heard me playing my Roth 1930 violin on a summer's afternoon, and he placed a hand-written invitation to tea on my door to discover who might be playing the Prelude and Allegro in the style of Paganini, by Fritz Kreisler. I responded favorably to the man's invitation. We enjoyed Lapsang Souchong tea and small cucumber sandwiches three days later in his study. There among the paraphernalia of an intellectual and musician of the old school, he allowed me to examine his exquisite Stradivarius.

Fiedler's conversation was full of allusions to his close friends among the American Neoclassical composers. He had just received new compositions from two of those, and he wanted my opinion about their suitability for the Valley Youth Symphony Orchestra. Naturally, I was pleased to discover the old man assumed without proof that I could sight-read a score. I gave him my affirmative response about the choices. As if discovering a talisman, my opinion opened our discussions to a wide range of subjects beyond music—to magic, for example, and the literary works of Thomas Mann. By the time his next student arrived, we were deep into Mann's works, whose original German versions were housed in their own bookcase.

I left the master violinist's row home with a renewed appreciation for the hidden talents situated within half a block of my own home. I had no idea we would ever meet again as we were both immured in our work.

From that time, I began to re-read Mann's greatest works, particularly *Doctor Faustus*, with deeper appreciation. Fiedler had convinced me that the German novelist had imbued his literary corpus with a mystical key to music appreciation. Ironically, the old man imparted this knowledge to me only two weeks before he suffered a terminal cardio-vascular accident and died. I felt lucky to have met the man before his demise, and I wondered how his passing would affect music in the Valley.

My friends Rochester and Spellman were well aware that Fiedler had died. They wanted to convene a séance to contact the spirit of the musician if only to gauge the maestro's own impression of his legacy. They had both enjoyed tea and cucumber sandwiches with the violinist. Their philosophical view of his passing left no room for tears or mourning since the man had only changed state as water becomes steam.

Discussing Dr. Fiedler as we drove the Studebaker to Philadelphia, I realized for the first time how *musical* my spectral friends were. Rochester was himself a violinist and Spellman a violist. Both had been musicians with the Philadelphia Symphony, and both had published music with E. C. Schirmer, to their credit. I narrowly missed being ensnared in a string quintet the two had formed. I simply had no extra time for the quintet, but I did agree to stand in from time to time for the second violinist in their group.

I returned from Philly with a stack of musical scores to practice for the quintet. I also returned with Spellman's theories about the profound meaning of music in the longer works of Thomas Mann. The more practical Rochester had no use for the novelist's word play. Music as a metaphor did nothing for his appreciation one way or another.

My own reading fell somewhere between the

opinions of my friends. Mann clearly loved music, but he also interweaved complex allusions to music in his novels, particularly in *Doctor Faustus*. I did not doubt Fiedler's idea that the novelist had extrapolated a grand theory of music in his works, but I loved Mann's writings with or without that knowledge.

I was reluctant to join Rochester and Spellman in their attempts to contact Fiedler's ghost in a séance. My reason was that the old man's ghost had come unbidden to me. The first time he materialized, he emerged from my peripheral vision looking sad and holding a replica of his Strad. I might have thought I was hallucinating, but Fiedler came in a neon blue figment two days later. His third appearance was in the Lehigh Parkway in a grotto. I began to suspect the virtuoso's spirit had become a general presence in the Valley.

Then, walking down North Eleventh Street, I heard the Stradivarius, distinctly. No other instrument had such a deep, resonant tone as that one. There was no mistaking it for anything else. I heard it on many occasions in places all over the Valley, but each time I heard the sound of that violin, I failed to locate its source. I thought of the immortal words of Keats: "Heard music is sweet, but that unheard is sweeter." No one else seemed to hear the music; perhaps, it came to me alone.

It did not take long for Fiedler's belongings to be removed and his row home to come on the housing market. By the time a new occupant had bought it and taken possession, the place had no vestige of the prodigy I had visited for tea. I had encountered Fiedler's spirit in so many places, I no longer associated it with North Eleventh Street specifically. I began to speculate about the man's legacy in terms of his abiding presence everywhere.

Rochester and Spellman were frustrated by their vain attempts to contact the spirit, and they had not observed its signs or heard the music from the man's violin as I had. I was hesitant to elaborate on what I had experienced for two reasons—I was not entirely sure I had not been deceiving myself and I did not want to make my friends jealous of special favors I was privy to.

I began to record my encounters with Fiedler in my diary. The music the invisible violin played was gradually changing from the Romantic classics to the Neoclassical modern scores. Many pieces were excellent compositions I had never heard before. I thought the spirit might be teasing me, but I composed what I heard in a deepening stack of scores. Over three dozen unidentified pieces had come to me in succession. I was now hearing no music that was familiar to me though the Strad was unmistakable.

I decided to take my stack of scores to a musicologist at the university for his opinion. Dr. Osculpian liked modern music, but he had never encountered anything like the samples I showed him. He suspected I had composed the works myself, but I attributed them to Fiedler but not to the unseen persona or ghost who played them so I could record them. The learned professor would never have believed my stories, and what was the use? If Fiedler was trying to convey his compositions from beyond the grave, I thought there was a better way to proceed.

After three months, I contacted Fiedler's executor to say I had in my possession fifty-odd original compositions by Dr. Fiedler. I said I might find others in the course of time. Ms. Alfred Fiedler Marsh, the executor, said she was not surprised. She told me others had contacted her about numerous extraneous compositions that had no tangible connections to her father's remains.

"Mr. Farnsworth, thank you for letting me know about the works you have found. Please make copies of the scores you have, and send the originals to me in a return envelope I shall be sending to you."

I did as Ms. Marsh directed. I also continued to write down the unheard music as it came to me. Once I received her receipt for the first package I had sent her, the sound of the Strad went silent. The dozen additional compositions that had been transcribed by me since I sent the first packet to Ms. Marsh I sent in a second envelope to the same address. I received thanks and reimbursement for my expenses. I felt I had done my duty to the memory of Dr. Fielder, whose virtual images I kept seeing by averted vision all over the Lehigh Valley.

Meanwhile, I played the music I had transcribed along with my standard repertoire though it was far too modern for my taste. In my second-floor music room, I sensed a presence whenever I played that music. I could not find evidence of a spirit lurking nearby, but the ghost of Fiedler was present.

Rochester and Spellman stopped by my row home to give me the good news: their quintet had been commissioned to perform selected unpublished works composed by Dr. Fiedler at a commemorative service in his honor in Philadelphia. Ms. Marsh had arranged for private publication of the selections, which would be edited by Dr. Osculpian.

The two specters had brought copies of the selections, which I recognized immediately as the identical submissions I had mailed to Ms. Marsh. My friends offered me the place of second violin in their quintet for the special concert, but I demurred since their regular second fiddle was available. I told them I would attend their commemoration and give them

119

hearty applause.

The date for the commemoration approached rapidly. The program, the score and the invitations were printed by one of the finer publishers in Philadelphia. My invitation arrived in the mail only one week prior to the event.

My friends and their entire quintet drove to the venue in the Studebaker. I drove down in my powder-blue Saab. Four hundred others had responded positively, and a respectable three hundred twenty showed up.

I was impressed by the speakers at the service. Ms. Marsh had done a fine job of pulling together the strands of the commemoration of her father. The quintet's performance was a *tour de force*, a credit to Rochester, Spellman and their three cohorts. In brief, I was not the only auditor standing to applaud the composer and the players.

The reception was exquisitely catered, with white wine and fine cheeses, Beluga caviar and toast points.

The press was well represented. A reporter for the *Philadelphia Inquirer* questioned as many people as possible about their memories of Dr. Fiedler. As I stood on the outside of the gathering, it took a long time for the reporter to reach me for an interview.

"My contact with Dr. Fiedler was limited to an afternoon tea at his home two weeks before his passing. I can only say, the man was unique in his musical contributions to the Lehigh Valley and his wide-reaching connections to the titans in the world music community on both sides of the Atlantic."

"Mr. Farnsworth, Ms. Marsh, Dr. Fiedler's daughter, told me you had possession of over fifty unpublished compositions that formed the piece that the quintet played this afternoon. As your time with Fiedler was limited, how do you account for such a large portion of his legacy being in your possession after his demise?"

"I understand a number of casual acquaintances had bits and pieces of Fiedler's musical legacy. My holdings were neither anomalous nor particularly large. Now if you will excuse me, I want to congratulate Mr. Rochester and Mr. Spellman on the fine performance of their quintet."

I pushed my way through the crowd to be with my friends for a minute before I departed for Allentown in my Saab. As I gave my valediction to my friends, I heard the music being played on the Stradivarius. I could not immediately find the source of the sound, but with averted vision, I found a specter seated on top of a pillar by the wall. I could see the spirit apply his bow, and I clearly heard the now-familiar unheard music. No one else seemed able to hear the sounds that I did. I decided it was time for me to leave the commemoration.

Driving home, I strained to hear the Strad, but I heard nothing but the tires on the highway. When I looked for a spirit, all I saw was the usual vision of cars speeding through the night into Philadelphia and out in two parallel, continuous streams.

I wondered about the final appearance of Dr. Fiedler at his own commemoration service. I thought his appearance might be a sign of approbation. In any case, Dr. Fiedler finally owned his posthumous compositions even if I was the only one to witness his mute confirmation. The Music Maser of North Eleventh Street had transcended the Valley through his death and, by circuitous means, made his works known eternally.

HIGH-DIVING MULES

The Lehigh Valley's animal rights activists had strenuous objections to the spectacle, but the high-diving mule act at the Monroe County Fair during the summers attracted large crowds even before the side show of the Banana Derby, featuring three pony-riding monkeys was added to attract newcomers and increase revenues.

On North Eleventh Street in Allentown, my next-door neighbors told me they attended the fair every year specifically to see the high-diving mules, but by the way they talked about the experience, their attitude was lackadaisical if not downright jaded. The valley natives tended to reduce every account to essentials, removing all elements of excitement or even interest from their expression.

According to their accounts, the storied mules would walk up a huge ramp, and, at the top, as they had evidently been trained to do, they would step off the ramp and fall into a six-foot-diameter circular pool of water directly below them. The only redemption in this bizarre routine was the cooling effect of the water in the sweltering summer heat.

At the entrance to the viewing tent, activists milled around incessantly, passing out leaflets and berating people who had paid to see the act, which was not a product of the valley at all. The enterprising man who managed and promoted the diving mules was a Floridian who genuinely believed P. T. Barnum's famous maxim, "There's a sucker born every minute."

Complementing Barnum's sentiment, comedian W. C. Fields coined the term, "Never give a sucker an even break!" as an ad lib in the musical *Poppy* in 1923, and subsequently as the title of a film he made in 1943.

The stolid Penn Dutch citizens of the valley would

have been mightily offended to be called a sucker. For them, the high-diving mules were merely part of the moving diorama of Valley Life.

Inevitably, Rochester and Spellman heard about the act. They had to see it for themselves. Accosted by the activists coming and going, they were plagued by guilt and remorse. They decided to discover whether the animals did suffer from their experiences. Inevitably, this line of thought led to mediated conversations with long-dead psychics like Annie Besant.

"Farnsworth," Spellman said, "we shall get to the bottom of this matter."

I was not sure how the two clairvoyants were going to do what they proposed. My concern was what they were going to do with their knowledge when they found it. The animal rights crowd would never countenance the idea that the animals did not care about their ordeal. If they did discover that cruel and unusual effects resulted from the diving act, commercial interests would surely debunk their "knowledge" as insubstantial and probably false.

Rochester seemed to read my mind: "What's the use? The mules are a local fixture now. Even if one of the mules was a Francis the Talking Mule, like the character in the Universal-International films of the 1950s, no one would believe it."

"Rochester, you may have hit on a solution."

"I have? Explain yourself."

"It has been almost seventy years since Francis the Talking Mule has been absent from the popular culture. Perhaps a revival of that character would open the opportunity for the mules to have their voice."

Spellman caught the drift in what I was suggesting. "We should make our pitch to Hollywood and let our findings about mules' feelings come out in an appropriately *mulish* comedy."

"Why not? NetFlix has done a lot worse."

My friends brooded on this idea for a while. Rochester said, "I suppose it would not hurt to gauge the filmic possibilities in parallel with our séances."

I was not included in every aspect of the two men's plan, but I did hear snippets as they progressed.

I recall that Spellman told me the shade of Annie Besant would not confirm communication between human and animal spirits. He had discovered the close alignment for the theosophist with vegetarianism in her *Vegetarianism in the Light of Theosophy*.

I also recall that Rochester had flown to Hollywood, only to be laughed out of a dozen film executive's offices talking about a revival of Francis the Mule.

Meanwhile, I did some reading about the origin of the animal rights movement. For example, I read Henry Stephens Salt's book *Animals' Rights: Considered in Relation to Social Progress* and Peter Singer's *Animal Liberation* among many others.

My heart told me we humans know precious little about the feelings of animals, and Dr. Jane Goodall, the English primatologist, was closest to knowing the truth. She was on the board of the Nonhuman Rights Project. In April 2002, she was named a UN Messenger of Peace. Goodall was an honorary member of the World Future Council. She was also a fully committed vegan.

From Goodall, I learned that not everything about "nature in the wild" is sweetness and light. A heartbreaking truth is that apes who are brutish and brutal attack and kill more intelligent and sensitive apes, cracking their skulls and eating them simply to show their "superiority." By extension, I reasoned making a mule climb to the top of a ramp and leap into a small vat of cold water might indeed be cruel. I regret not having discussed this with Dr.Goodall before her death.

It occurred to me that the spirit of Goodall might be a superior spirit source than Annie Besant for the animal research we were doing. So I suggested to Rochester and Spellman the possibility of a séance with Jane Goodall's ghost. My friends were wholeheartedly in favor of this idea and moved right away to conduct their séance.

At the same time, Rochester learned that his pitch in Hollywood had subsequently generated significant interest in a revival of Francis the Talking Mule. In fact, one of the executives had asked him to return to California to discuss the prospect with a team of his script writers for money.

When he told me about this fortuitous turn of events, I said, "By all means, go! Spellman can conduct the séance with Goodall. If you pave the way for injecting his findings in a segment of the Francis the Mule pilot, we shall have achieved our objectives."

"I feel a little guilty making money in Tinseltown while you and Spellman do the hard work of teasing out the message on this side of the country in Philadelphia."

"You made the Hollywood contact, and you generated the interest. No one else can take your place as our connection to the film industry."

"Since you put it that way, I'll go. But what idea should I insert in the pilot? I have never worked with script writers before. You are the professional writer, so you should help me out."

"What you need is a placeholder. Why not pitch a séance about animal cruelty focusing on mules?"

"I get it. Yes, that should work."

Rochester flew back to California on an expense account. Spellman and I rode in the Studebaker to the Masonic Hall where we used our medium to contact

125

the spirit of Jane Goodall.

The famous primatologist's spirit was every bit as gracious in death as she had been in life. There was only one problem.

"Young men, I am flattered you are asking my opinion, but I was a primatologist. Your research is focused on a quadruped, a close relative to both the horse and the donkey. You probably want to summon the shade of a horse whisperer like Buck Brannaman instead of me."

Spellman shook his head. "Dr. Goodall, you are the most brilliant analyst of the feelings of other species in their interactions with humans. Perhaps you can tell us whether a chimpanzee would feel it cruel and unusual treatment if he or she was subjected to the same treatment as the high-diving mules we have told you about."

Goodall's spirit laughed. "They would be throwing their own feces at their trainer and doing everything possible to reverse the situation with the humans involved. You also mentioned something about three monkeys riding ponies in a side show along with the high-diving mules. That is more the chimpanzee's speed."

After the séance, Spellman was all for interviewing Buck Brannaman, but I prevailed upon him to call Rochester and tell him the results of our Goodall encounter. I also suggested that he let his friend know a figure like Brannaman should figure in the Hollywood séance about contacting the spirit of a mule. Only after he had done what I advised did we try to reach the horse whisperer.

Since he had been the inspiration for a book and a film as well as his own documentary titled *Buck*, the great man was extremely busy and had little time for us. He did grant us five minutes of his time wherein we told him about the high-diving mules and asked his opinion.

"Cruel and unusual? I'll say that ordeal would be a form of torture for the mules. In fact, I believe legal proceedings should commence immediately against the mule's owner and trainer. I will fax you a template to use to file your legal brief. If I were in your vicinity, I would probably make a visit to ensure the man never even thought of having another show of that kind."

When we terminated our call, we had the best evidence possible for the cruelty argument. Fortunately we had recorded Brannaman's words, which we played in their entirety for Rochester.

"I will tell the writing team about the comments of the horse whisperer tomorrow. I will also suggest that the team bring aboard Brannaman as a consultant. I think we agree that our message will have authority as well as the best possible delivery Hollywood can give it."

The producer of the new Francis the Mule was impressed with Rochester's recommendation. As a consequence, the producer fired Rochester as redundant while he brought Brannaman aboard as chief consultant. Rochester was free to return to Pennsylvania. When he returned, we treated him to dinner at the Dutch Diner where he told the whole story of his gig with the studio system.

"We have the best possible result. I do not care to be involved as long as our ideas are in the pilot program." Spellman and I were grateful our friend was a good sport. We followed the progress of *Francis the Talking Mule II* in the shadows. The pilot turned out as well as could be expected. Eventually to avoid a potential lawsuit, the high-diving mules had to be replaced by the 20-mule team for Borax, "the natural laundry detergent booster and multi-purpose cleaner." Borax became a primary sponsor of the pilot program, so even the implication that animal rights was involved had to be scrapped in the re-scripting exercise that followed.

Buck Brannaman called us as soon as he learned about the studio's deal with Borax. "I suppose you have heard about the gutting of our program. I am resigning from the production team and withdrawing my name as an advisor. The studio is happy about my departure as I was making too many waves about animal rights. I don't know what they are going to do to achieve verisimilitude now, and fortunately I don't have to care. Anyway, thank you for plugging me into the game. If only humans could listen as well as horses, things might have been otherwise."

Rochester, Spellman and I decided to visit the high-diving mule act at the Monroe County Fair. No one who was there knew our history with the effort to promote animal rights. So on the way in, we were importuned by the animal rights activists. We witnessed the Banana Derby and saw how the three monkeys were throwing their feces at the trainer just as Goodall had said they would. A small dog accompanied the mules to the top of the long, sloping ramp. The mules dropped into the pool, one after the other. Then it was time for us to run the gauntlet of activists again.

When the Studebaker dropped me off at my row home, my next-door neighbors were lounging on their front porch.

"Mr. Farnsworth, have you heard the good news?"

"You will have to tell me what has happened. You are always the first to know."

"There's going to be a new Francis the Mule series, and the pilot is looking much better than the old one. It is going to premier tonight on Netflix. Will you be tuning in?"

"Now that you have informed me about the premier, I guess I will try to see it. We can compare notes on the pilot tomorrow if you like."

"I don't know why Hollywood decided to remake that old series, but I'm very glad they are doing it. Mules are smarter than most humans, you know. And what the high-diving mules are doing demeans them. Can you believe Borax is sponsoring the entire series?"

"I couldn't agree more about demeaning the mules. I wonder how many household use Borax. Have a good evening listening to the police band radio."

"We will do just that. Good night."

As I prepared for bed after viewing the travesty of the pilot program, I thought through the exercise my friends and I had endured in pursuit of justice for the high-diving mules. We had not exactly done what we intended, but we had learned a lot in the process and accomplished much that we had not even thought of. The 1950s-era show would translate well to the current generation. People had not evolved much in seventy years. The twenty-mule-team cleanser was needed more than ever. Maybe, I thought, *Francis the Talking Mule II* will serve a good purpose. Humans should know the animals around them may have secret powers of problem-solving that exceed those of our species.

DECEPTIVE CADENCE

Symphony of celestial light and sound
The sand hill cranes wading swelling king tide
Fallen earth harbors squidgy swampy ground
Where once fish leapt sparkling as they elide.
The twilight mingles shadows with the shades
As we bemoan our worries on the pier
Small matters blown like reeds of everglades
Beckoning ghosts and cold thoughts of the bier.
Why so sad as the heavens open wide?
So young you seem against the Pleiades.
I am the aged one whose numbers slide
Towards the yawning void of grim Hades.
Once I ruled unwisely with scepter crude,
Unruly seas I sought by sway to quiet.
You witnessed that folly and wept and smiled.
Ignoble spells failed to quell the riot.
So hubris always falls by sleight beguiled.
Shut the window and draw the heavy drape.
Think not reverses time can overturn.
We made our mortal measures to escape
In vain as wretched creatures born to burn.
To rise above the sea that lays us low,
Take now my hand and match me as I go.
Your weeping beggars what we've done below
In heat and now we change from fast to slow
And as we soar, let's revel in the glow
Of our sonic memorial echo.

VENOM

My gloved hands move among African grays.
Chirping crickets spring from stingers in fright.
Scorpions arthropods hunt nights, sleep days
While I milk their venom in cool blue light.
Why not herpetology for end time?
Blind eyes scanning as they coiled, struck and struck.
White squirts in spirits with a squeeze of lime:
Empty fangs still only hurt, with good luck.
My lure to arachnids instead was gain:
Pure gallons each for thirty-nine millions.
Overcoming ancient fears with no pain
With risks reduced and supplies of billions.
I a wriggler stretch its barbed sting;
A single liquid drop's my profiting.

INCISORS MINDING

Your slippery mouth and tongue invade my sleep
I writhe but cannot rise as I am bound
Along the slimy ground I slowly creep
While you devour, your chewing makes no sound.
How long I'll wait, I cannot estimate
So, terrified, despair I where I lie,
Your meal delectable and consummate
Halloween treat *and* trick for me to die.
I said no prayers before I ventured in.
Nor did I look for you but me you snared.
Others may moan when mired in baleful sin
I thought I might escape—but your teeth bared.
So like this Eve, I feel the Devil's due
Incisors minding flesh without a clue.

BLACK ROSE, BLOOD PEN

Surprise upon my bedspread: one black rose,
Not wine or blood dark, but lamp wick's soot black,
Long-stemmed yet touching that to catch its nose,
Thorns sharp pierced. I bled free and shook it back.
Thus princess matched fat king's majestic mind:
Crimson drops penned Marge's cryptic sign:
Knights of order sharp, new with rapiers lined,
Invitation to clandestine design.
Could black rose royal summons mystic be?
Or might it be that high lad seeks low love?
Why not both Lord's weapon and red bloods' fee
Should close below still matrix soul above.
Although I weep and bleed, black rose I know:
His love quills blood on my chaste pillow.

ST. VALENTINE'S DAY'S NO MASSACRE

You, Ariadne, fancy sanguine sport?
Chocolates and flowers seem inadequate?
Well, let's dine on blue stakes at the stockyard,
My slaughtered heart squeezed by your tentacles.
The vaunted saint enables nuptial rites,
But we struggle for labyrinthine thrills.
Your father will channel golden candles;
Your mocking smile will palliate my grief.
I see you vault high over my wide horns.
Your small hands press on my massive shoulders,
Your back arches and your toes point skyward,
As Theseus fingers your thread amazed.
My rival wins your faith and sails away;
I fall as prelude for your deity.

BLOOD RED VALENTINE

Suitors by scores your savage scorn makes bleed
Though you remain aloof, imperious.
My billets' bullets fly as shrapnel screed
As they fall short in fields inglorious.
Your matchless eyes are steely adamants
Not marking blood of victims you have slain.
I know your cruel joy at supplicants,
Prisoners whose wails your wiles contain.
When will you truce proclaim? Is your red heart
Bent on destruction to the last man's head
I raised my siege, so I have done my part.
I would withdraw from red fields of the dead.
Yet linger I to read your Valentine
To move your mind and make you alone mine.

NO KISSING

Public displays are verboten this week.
Outrage is campus fashion, with panache.
Ophelias yearn as brooding Hamlets seek.
Didos queue for pyres of consuming ash.
Invert the glass, and time pursues the past.
Genders blend in forming Mobius plays,
As if a tutor's dry lessons might last
More than this semester's quester's lays.
Time was, I wrote all ladies' fulsome praise.
Odes I scribed when dear Flossie was delight.
Now in the Ratskeller I schooners raise,
Not cowed, but waiting for the waning right.
Why do we gyre, yet recapitulate?
Lysistrata cries, but stays much too late.

CUT SHORT ON THE SHORT CUT

Taking the short cut across pumpkin fields,
The two stepped over vines by moonlight.
In the distance were sounds of high jinks and cat-calls,
Furtive, costumed creatures acting out the night.
"Come on, Francis, we'll be late-—hell's to pay,"
"You go on ahead, Sis. I won't be late."
Alone now, Becky heard heard her friends' wild play,
Or so she thought. She pressed through the far gate.
"Francis, the zombies! They are eating me!"
Her brother had problems of his devising.
He fell, and vines took life and reached for him.
He heard his sister's frantic screams, then nothing.
"I don't think shortcuts are a good idea," he cried.
Rotting choked him as hooded death's scythe sliced.

DEEP BLACK WATER

On the edge of the void, she lost her mind,
Fell and her hand hit rows of framed prints
Glass everywhere and when she came to
Blood all over the hall, an emergency call
And back to the hospital for another romp.
Tentacle rigs with lights, beeps and sirens,
A room in a ward, buffed linoleum floors
Polishers whining and low sounds paging
Occasional screams. Are they yours?
Again on the edge of the void, she drowses.
New spring flowers, and poems from sad poets,
Laughter along the long passages with footsteps,
Empty pedestrian greetings and hollow smiles.
A tentacle cuff squeezes hard then releases
"You could not wait to get back here?"

Not her physician but the hospitalist,
Orchestrator of the institutional horror,
Her retinue like a Greek chorus dancing,
Her hands are butterflies. Escape? Perhaps,
But where? And for how long? Narcotic sleep?
None from outside come. Shades always drawn,
Level by level she descends, not really caring,
And who should know on what ledge she waits
Finally tucked in her coma? Infinite questions
With answers composed in deep black water.

HER WILD RIDE ON HALLOWEEN

Jill hated her brother for everything,
But tonight she was free to ride.
Picked up at home in costume,
She sat by the scythe-man.

They drove south across the border.
El Paso was far too tame.
They stopped in a desert cemetery.
Death gave her tequila.

She knocked back the bottle and laughed.
He eyed her bare legs and said,
"Pull down your panties and pull up your skirt."
She slapped him. He slugged her.

She was angry but needed his car,
So she smiled and looked at her shoes.
He repeated, "Pull down your panties and pull up your
skirt."
He threatened with his scythe.
She slowly did as he asked
But left her track shoes on.
He forced a weird rictus
When she was nearly naked.
He opened his car's trunk.
She saw a dead princess's body
In a pink tutu and dancing shoes
White and turning blue.

Jill stumbled toward the road.
Death followed, waving his scythe.
She was naked in track shoes.
She was not laughing as he was.
When he reached for her,

She kicked for his groin
But caught his thin leg.
It came off as he fell.
A pile of folding bones,
He groped for her.
She kicked his hand off.
She stripped off his black robe

Jill wrapped herself in his robe.
She went back to his car.
She turned the key
And took off driving like hell.

She crossed the border,
Not stopping for ICE.
Two policemen followed.
They pulled her over.
They wore Anon masks.
They had drawn their weapons.
She did not wait but
Pressed pedal to metal.

She drove straight home.
Her bro was there.
He laughed at her disguise
And admired her shoes.
He let her into the house.
She sashayed to her room.
There she took off the robe
And stood by the mirror

Where she saw a bony skeleton,
No meat on her bones.
Just two new track shoes
Kept her from being nude.

She heard bro answer the door.
He let two people in.
Trick-or-treaters from Sinaloa
Looking only for her.
They burst into her bedroom
And saw her standing,
Looking familiarly naked.
She smiled and posed.
Those two young men
Died suddenly, and then
Bro slouched at her door.
"You didn't warn them?"
"No need. They know now.
Their pal is at the cemetery
In Ciudad *JUÁREZ*.
He almost raped me."
"Better almost raped than almost escaped."
They laughed for a minute.
She lit two cigarettes.
He brought them a bottle.

The two drank till midnight.
Then he walked out,
And she walked out.
They drove through the morning.

THE TRANSFORMATION

Dark thoughts emerge this evening dank with dew,
Racking his mind with anguish hour by hour.
As black hairs crowd his back, he feels new power.
Spittle foams his mouth, red where sharp teeth grew.
The moon is full. His time will be midnight.
His savage claws will rake a human heart.
Wolf's fangs will tear raw flesh from bone apart.
Hot breath fogs his glass and reddens his sight.
The transformation hurries for his feast;
His feet and hands swell with nails and paws.
Gnathions elongate along his jaws.
Pain radiates as he becomes the beast.
The snarling werewolf steals along the street.
Woe to humans he chances to meet.

VIRIDIAN HUNGER

You flee from me, yet you cannot
Ever defeat our master Death.
His scythe is our common comfort.
You protest, my love, that you cannot
Love me? That you would flee?
How can you say you do not love me?
We are now bound to our dying days.
One touch, and we are wed, we two.
You look for something human, food?
And I look for human hosts as food.
My love is indiscriminate and pure.
I will have all of you, or none.
Besides, you must consider how I grow.
I fester, eat and swell and make heat.
Your fever tells me that you love.
No love you will ever know is more
Complete or perfect. I am entirely yours.
I am so bound to you I exude in sweat
And when your blood boils, I vent.
You eat where I lurk and I find you
Wanting, while I hungering do
For you what you would do—if you knew
That midnight adventures are no better
Than my invasion of your primordial guts.
My invisible teeth tear at your cells.
Insatiable, I become sated one by one.
Your immune systems are woefully weak.
Your habits are deplorable except
You let me in so easily, and I die happy
In my feast on you, which lasts until we die.
Your defenses are without effect.
I am the virus that will with my millions
Of brothers invade and kill, and then
Jump to your loved ones and your best

Defenders who know nothing of me.
They have no defense against me.
I eat and multiply. You stand and wait.
You cannot find me, and I love to hide.
Ease of entry. Ease of passage. My treat.
Heated body, yours, my best advantage.
So easy it is to get the food I need.
And you, the food, are so easy, so easy.
Viridian rapture, hear it now? The sound
Of wracking pain and headache
Of wailing, primordial wailing
Of waiting, perspiring, raving.
You know—or will know—my signs. I am
Viridian love, whose crypt lies in your bones.

ABOUT THE AUTHOR

E. W. Farnsworth, an Ohio writer, has won many prizes for his tales of the paranormal and cosmic horror generally. Yet he is also known for his Westerns, spy stories and detective fiction as well as science fiction.

The following list of his publications with AudioArcadia.com will indicate the range of his writings (from the latest at the top to the most remote):

SOURCES FOR E.W. FARNSWORTH'S OTHER WORKS OF HORROR

'Mobile Dusters,' *Psychopomps: Shepherds of the Dead Anthology,* edited by Cindy Grigg, Misch Masch Publishing September 2015. Out of Print. Author Interview with Cindy Grigg 2015

Tales from the Grave Anthology, Zimbell House Publishing, September 2015.
https://www.amazon.com/Tales-Grave-Ghostly-Collection-Stories/dp/1942818122

'The Black Marble Griffon' and Other Disturbing Tales, Zimbell House Publishing, October 2016. https://www.amazon.com/Black-Marble-Griffon-Other-Disturbing/dp/1942818955

'Locked in Public Storage on Halloween,' *Curse of the Hallow Moon Anthology* EdingleIndieHouse, October 2021.
https://www.amazon.com/Curse-Hallow-Moon-Halloween-Anthology-ebook/dp/B09JKZJZYB

'The Halloween Séances,' *Halloween 2022 Blame It on the Pumpkin Anthology* DreamPunk Press, October 2022.
https://www.amazon.com/Blame-Pumpkin-Pamela-K-Kinney/dp/1954214162#:~:text=Enjoy%20these%208%20scary%20stories,Jennifer%20Kyrnin%2C%20Greg%20Partic k%2C%20S.%20P.

Made in the USA
Middletown, DE
06 September 2023

38123952R00086